TIN

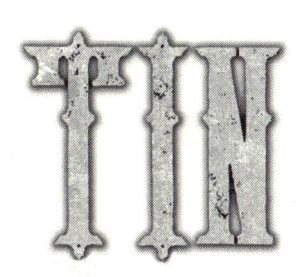

The Grave Knights
Book 2

International Bestselling Author
M. Merin

All Rights Reserved.

By the U.S. Copyright Act of 1976, the scanning, uploading, and electronic sharing of any part of this book without permission of the publisher is unlawful piracy and theft of the author's intellectual property. This book or any portion thereof may not be reproduced or used in any manner whatsoever without the express written permission of the author except for brief quotations used in a book review.

This book is a work of fiction. The names, characters, places, and incidents are products of the writer's imagination or have been used fictitiously, and are not to be construed as real. Any resemblance to actual persons, living or dead, events, locales, or organizations is entirely coincidental.

The use of actors, artists, movies, TV shows and song titles/lyrics throughout this book are done so for storytelling purposes and should in no way be seen as an advertisement. Trademark names are used editorially with no intention of infringement of the respective owner's trademark.

This book is intended for adults only. Contains sexual content and language that may offend some. The suggested reading audience is 18 years or older. I consider this book Adult Romance due to language and sexual situations.

Thank you for respecting the hard work of this author.

Published in the United States of America.

Tin: Grave Knights MC Book 2 (A Mayhem Makers Book)

Copyright 2023 Maura O'Brien

Photography: Brenda Keller, Stillhouse Images

Cover Model: Christopher W.

Cover: CT Cover Creations

Editing: Erin Toland of Edits by Erin

Formatting: Dark Water Covers

MOTORCYCLES, MAFIA, AND MAYHEM EVENT DISCLAIMER

This book is a work of fiction that was created as a multi-author collaboration to tie-in to a reader event and not a representation of actual events. I didn't get to mention every author I wanted to and thought it best to change the name of my – again – fictional readers who interact with my characters.

NOTE

In my first several RBMC, Flagstaff Chapter books, Joey's father's MC is referred to as the Hades Knights. I never planned on a spin-off, but in the years between me writing **Axel** and then starting this book for the MMM signing, that fictional title was used by another author and I decided to alter the name of Parker King's MC to avoid confusion. So, for those of you who were paying attention, remember this fictional world has to be fluid sometimes.

CHARACTER LIST

Parker King – road name Me'ansome which is a Cornish phrase - a mother's endearment for a male child. He has twins from a previous relationship.

Tin – Long time friend of Parker and VP of the Grave Knights.

Joey – Parker's daughter who was raised by her mother's family. Married to Axel Saint, of the Royal Bastards. (Axel: Royal Bastards MC, Flagstaff Chapter, Book 1)

Tommy/Ransom – Joey's twin brother who was raised by Parker.

Axel – VP of the RBMC, Flagstaff Chapter. (Axel: Royal Bastards MC, Flagstaff Chapter, Book 1)

Declan – President of the RBMC, Flagstaff Chapter. (Declan: Royal Bastards MC, Flagstaff Chapter, Book 2)

CHARACTER LIST

Red – Tin's older brother and a member of the RBMC, Flagstaff Chapter.

Diesel – IT and Security for the RBMC, Flagstaff Chapter and its holdings. (Diesel: Royal Bastards MC, Flagstaff Chapter, Book 3)

Wolfman – He handles wet work for the MC. (Wolfman: Royal Bastards MC, Flagstaff Chapter, Book 5)

Piper Kyle – IT consultant with an identical twin sister that she covers for during MMM. (Me'ansome: The Grave Knights, Book 1)

Paige Kyle - Self-published romance author, thief, and con-woman – Piper's identical twin.

Tober – Piper and Paige's cousin.

Felix – Tober, Piper, and Paige's cousin.

Betta – Tober's mother.

Tiff – Piper and Paige's great-aunt.

Earl – Tiff's son.

Nick – Earl's son.

ONE

Tin

"Fucking twins, man!" King tells me the moment I pick up his call.

"You don't say," I answer, grimacing at the double take I had just experienced.

Sitting in my SUV, I'm watching a woman whose face I know quite well, crawl out of a second floor window before pulling a backpack out behind her and cautiously lowering the ladder of the rickety old fire escape. "Did Piper happen to mention that her sister is her *identical* twin sister?"

"Yeah, I told you that," he answers. "Did you hear me? The ultrasound says Piper and me are having twins. Joey and Ransom are going to go nuts."

"They aren't the only ones," I sigh, doubting I would have missed a detail like Piper having a mirror image. Hell, I would have been out the door and tracking her down instantly, if I had any inkling there were two of them.

Last spring, this long-dead heart of mine actually skipped a beat when I first laid eyes on Piper. Unfortunately, she was already wrapped in Me'ansome's embrace that night and while I like to tell him that she's only with him because he met her first, we all know that isn't true.

I'm not foolish enough to think that a soulmate exists in this world, but I have to say, after seeing those two together, I've never seen people more in sync with each other.

When Parker is running hot, Piper calms him down and I can't count the number of times I've seen them unconsciously reaching out to each other, threading their fingers together at the same moment.

The ladder catches on something, dangling at least six feet from the ground and I get out of my truck to go and help Piper's twin sister, but the girl starts down before I can signal her. By the time I'm under the fire escape, she releases her grip, not accounting for the weight of her pack and falls backwards.

Air escapes her lungs on impact, but she doesn't seem to be hurt.

"Or you could have waited a minute," I say, crossing my arms as I stand over her.

Her large brown eyes nearly bulge out of her sockets and I'm sure she would have screamed if the wind hadn't been knocked out of her when she landed.

"If you didn't give the impression that you were in a bit of a hurry, I'd tell you to take a breath, Paige." The use of her name helps to focus her attention on my face before her eyes shift down to my cut. "Piper said she was worried about you, I had other business out this way, so her Old Man asked that I check in on you."

Reaching down, I help her to her feet, even as she still struggles to breathe, and I turn her in the direction of my truck to get her moving. Hell if I know why she opted to take that crappy old fire escape, but I sure as fuck know trouble when I see it and Paige is most likely shown in the dictionary under that word.

The contrast between her and Piper is not lost on me for a second, from the world-weary look in her eyes to the way she wears her hair.

"Old man," she gasps out, interrupting my thoughts. "That's what I've heard he is, alright. And what kind of name is Me'ansome?"

"Now, now. Us older men prefer the term, well-seasoned." I chuckle as I open the passenger door and try to grab her backpack as she jumps in, but she holds tight to it as she throws a glare over her shoulder at me and I hold my hands up in surrender. "You can thank me later, but what do you say we get out of here?"

"You really know how to sweep a girl off her feet, don't'ya?" she asks with a laugh as she pops open the container of gum on my center console and tosses a couple of pieces into her mouth.

"Why don't you give your sister a call? She's been worried about you," I tell her and can't miss the side-eye she gives me.

"Can I use your phone?" she asks, throwing a wide smile in my direction.

"Fuck, no," I quickly answer.

"Why not?"

"Because you are shady as fuck and I ain't letting you near anything with my personal data on it."

The bitch throws her head back, laughing. Christ, I'm going to be in for it with this one. And my excitement over finding out Piper is a twin swirls down the drain as I remember how different Parker and his, thankfully now, deceased twin brother were.

"Are you gonna to tell me where we're heading?"

"I've got to get up north of Fresno, then we'll

head back to Utah. Once I drop you off at your sister's, where you go is up to you," I tell her, looking over at her tanned thighs and wondering when Daisy Dukes became a thing again.

"Fresno, huh? What's up there?"

"A man I have to talk to," I answer, grinning at the tight line her mouth stretches into when I give her a non-answer. This could be fun. "How do you not have a car?"

"I have a car," she snaps back. "It's just not in California."

"Where is it? Or did you lose it?"

"You're kind of a dick. I mean the whole shaved head look works for you, but you should focus on developing your personality," she informs me, as if the daggers she's sending my way aren't already relaying her opinion of me.

"I don't need a fucking life coach." It's my turn to get annoyed with her.

"I have been told by lots of people that I would be a great life coach, thank you. I do, however, write romance novels and I'm pretty certain you could get a lot of women if you were a little nicer," she informs me, peering around to the back seat.

"I get plenty of women, if I were nicer they'd want to stick around. Besides, I'm not taking advice from someone that I just caught sneaking out of some apartment."

"It wasn't an apartment. It was the business office for the pawn store on the first floor of that building." She lets that gem slip as she starts digging through the cooler she located behind her seat, giving me a great view of her ass since she's kneeling on her seat.

"Fuck, what the hell's in your bag," I ask, reaching across the armrest to snag it. That gets her attention quick, and she kicks it out of my reach, spinning to get her ass back in place.

"That's none of your business and nothing that doesn't belong to me," Paige snaps, utterly unconvincing.

"Yeah? Did it belong to you when you woke up this morning, or do you have some recent acquisitions? I swear, if you do anything to get me disbarred, it won't matter that you're Piper's sister, I will lose my shit," I tell her, wishing there was a good spot to pull over and dump out her bag. That or take her over my knee for a few good smacks.

"Like an actual lawyer, or like you blackmailed some registrar with a gambling problem to add you to the rolls?"

"And what, I sold off some stolen organs to

scrounge together the money to bribe people to go and take the bar exams for me?" I scoff at her.

"That's how my uncle got his law degree," she mumbles and my jaw drops open in surprise. "I mean the gambling scenario, not the black-market organ trade."

"Christ. I went to an actual school. I studied. I took the bar in four states," I say, feeling the need to be very specific considering the turn the conversation has taken.

"Here," she says, and my eyes shift down to see her holding out a dollar. "Now you're my lawyer."

"That's actually not how retainers work," I answer her, but toss the buck into the compartment with the rest of my change from fast food places and whatnot.

"So, you want to know what's in my bag?" Paige asks, giving me a smug smile.

"I don't. I am curious about how you misplaced your car, especially since it required me to drive completely out of my way to come rescue your ass."

"Rescue might be too extreme a term," she muses, taking a sip of water. "And I didn't misplace my car. I had gotten a ride to Los Angeles with a friend of a cousin of mine. Unfortunately, he was becoming decidedly less friendly. So yesterday morning, I reached out to Piper to see if she could come get me."

"Really, you thought dragging her into your shenanigans was a good idea?"

"*Shenanigans?*" she parrots back to me, reaching up in an attempt to yank my sunglasses off. "How old are you?"

"Old enough to know that someone who's over four months pregnant, shouldn't be tasked to drive across a couple of states to deal with whatever scam you're running," I answer, smacking my temple on the window as I dodge her hand all while trying to keep the truck from swerving. "Knock it off or I'm tying you up and tossing you in the back."

I don't look at her for a moment, until I realize that she's not even going to attempt a response to either of my statements, and when I do, I instantly see that her tan skin is flushed red and her eyes are filling with tears. What the fuck just happened?

Training my eyes back on the road, I try to wait her out, but nearly ten minutes go by before I hear a silent sob and that's when I know I have to say something.

"Um, are you alright?" I ask, getting a bitter sounding laugh in return.

"No," she answers, not giving me anything to go on, so we sink back into silence.

I'm at a loss so I decide to treat her like anyone else. I turn on the radio and get comfortable in my seat. She'll talk when she's ready.

Paige

What an asshole!

I'm obviously not alright and about thirty seconds after finding out that my sister is halfway through her first pregnancy, I realized I don't even know this guy's name.

There was something on his cut, but I had barely caught my breath before he was shoving me into his truck and it has been a whirlwind since then.

My phone's been dead for a day or so, something I regularly let happen when I'm running an errand for my family. It makes it harder for people to find me that way; of course, it sucks ass when I actually need to call someone.

I know I've been busy, but Piper is my everything and that she hasn't let me know that she's pregnant is breaking my heart.

Fuck. The signing in Houston was only, shit—well, that pumpkin spice shit is everywhere so it's probably early fall now, and I calculate how far along she could be considering she met Me'ansome at the end of May. I debate asking the man next to me how far out we are from Thanksgiving, but he already has pegged me as 'sketchy'.

Laughing to myself, I shake my head at that. Piper walks the straight and narrow, but next to the rest of our family, I'm practically Snow White. Well, maybe Snow is a slight exaggeration, doesn't she have a slightly adventurous friend? Who's that Rose Red character?

My eyes slide to the left again as I consider how to move forward with this man, but when I notice him squeezing and relaxing his fingers on the wheel, I realize he has no clue how to deal with me either.

"There's only one thing that can make this more awkward," I say, breaking the silence then waiting until I have his full attention. "I have no idea what your name is."

That gets a chuckle out of him and I smile wryly at him in return. "I'm serious. Here I am in your vehicle, you're racing your ass up the highway, and I have no fucking idea what name to gasp out when the hotel cleaning lady finds me bleeding out in the morning."

"Sorry to break it to ya, sweets. I got a vacation rental, so there won't be a cleaning lady coming to your rescue."

"That honeyed tongue of yours gets all the ladies,

doesn't it?" I ask him, batting my eyelashes in his direction.

"I'm Tin," he finally answers me.

"Is that your first or last name?"

"Neither," he grunts out. "You doing better?"

"Considering I just found out that I'm going to be an auntie from an absolute stranger, who might murder me later," I try to answer in my usual upbeat sarcastic manner, when another sob cuts me off and I wave my hand in the air as I turn to stare out of my window again.

Once I feel a little more in control of myself, I take a deep breath and consider the man beside me; deciding that I don't mind that he doesn't pressure me to talk when I'm upset. I mean, if I was going to be completely honest with Tin, I'd tell him it's nice having a moment to collect my thoughts.

"Since we have a couple of hours on this highway, can I charge my phone?" is my next question, indicating the map showing our progress on his console.

He gives me a nod, our fingers touching when we both reach for the USB cord makes my breath hitch. For the tenth time since we got on the road, I catch him looking at my upper thighs again before he looks at my face.

"I'm just gonna keep this away from you," he says, unplugging his phone and sliding it into his pocket, while I have the perfect angle to see he's winking at me, regardless of his reflective sunglasses.

I startle awake and turn to my left, needing a second to figure out where I am as the truck hits a pothole.

"I unplugged your phone about twenty minutes ago, it should be good though," Tin says quietly. "I needed to know where to go once I got off the highway."

"Do you mind if I snag one of your energy drinks?" I ask, needing something to get my brain clicking again. Unlike last time, I wait for his nod of permission before I turn around and grab my favorite brand out of his cooler. "Want one?"

"I'll take the ginger ale," he responds, continuing on before I can mock him over that choice. "Tomorrow, I've got work to do then I want to get on the road before midnight. Depending on the traffic around Vegas, I can get you to your sister in time for breakfast."

"Vegas?" I squeak out, my heartbeat instantly skipping even before my first sip of the drink. "Can we go another way?"

"Not without it taking twice as long through the

mountains and national parks," he grounds out. "So, no."

"Oh, but that sounds like it would be really pretty and scenic." Alright, that is not my best work, but it would be really bad if I ended up dead before seeing Piper again.

"Yeah, I was right about you. Sketchy as fuck."

"Is that a 'maybe', at least?" I ask, nearly in pain from biting my tongue to stop myself from blurting out my typical sarcastic response. "And I believe you said I was 'shady', somehow 'sketchy' sounds worse."

Even though he doesn't answer, I figure I still have a chance of winning this conversation as he pulls into the driveway of a cute little townhouse and I get excited at the sight of the pool I spot across the parking lot. Now I know what I'll be doing tomorrow while he's working.

"Let's check this place out, then we'll go grab dinner," Tin says as he slides out of his seat and stretches out his back; I swear I hear each joint pop. Well-seasoned, indeed.

Walking through the unit, I'm kind of relieved and surprised that he got a three-bedroom place, then I remember what he said about leaving tomorrow night.

"Wait, how many nights did you rent this for?" I ask him before he ducks into the master bedroom.

"Two."

"But we're only staying here one night," I say, trying to figure out what his deal is.

"My credit card will say two nights, plus if we take all those side roads you mentioned, there'll be fewer cameras tracking us on the highway. Now, you can't even complain about the long-ass trip home, because it was your idea," he says, finally taking off his sunglasses and grinning at me. "I'm going to jump online and find a steakhouse, be ready to go in twenty minutes."

"What if I'm a vegetarian?" I blurt out.

"You can order a salad."

With that he closes the bedroom door, not even giving me a second to get my thoughts together.

Fuck.

He's a total fucking psychopath.

It's not vanity when I say that I'm hot. From the time I was twelve years old, boys and some creepy-ass men, were sniffing around me. They were the perfect foil to try out the skills my mom and aunts had been teaching me since childhood. Well, both Piper and me, but they quickly got tired of her lecturing them that lying and stealing was bad.

We were mainly taught sleight of hand and three-card monte with some other basic cons thrown in, but still, my family always said that I had that little extra spark that made people do what I wanted them to do. And it was true. If I want a man to do what I want, he will.

Except this one has me all crosswire. And I'll have to figure out how to watch my mouth, my back, and my score over the next few days, all without leading anyone back to Piper.

Christ, Piper can barely tell a lie without turning bright red or breaking into a sweat but give that girl a couple of paper clips and there's not a door that she can't unlock. Not that she'll put her God-given talents to use for any of us.

I may have been safer finding my way back to her on my own, not that I'm ungrateful that she sent out the cavalry when she received the last text from me.

Our family has been coming down harder on us since we turned eighteen, expecting us to pull our weight with their scores. Unbeknownst to them, Piper made her own plans and flew the coop, two minutes after we graduated from high school.

It was zero surprise that she got a full scholarship to college, with her grades and all; it was surprising that she managed to line it all up without our family finding out. She begged me to go with her, painting her typically rosy picture of the little apartment we could get off-campus while we work regular jobs.

Piper was determined that we could break away from our family, but I knew better. I packed her things up, put my lifesavings in her backpack and dropped her off at the train station. One of us could go, but if we both left, they would have tracked our asses down and dragged us back.

I never had any illusions about what my life would be like, at least until the summer we turned twenty-one. We had a great-aunt that was the stuff of legends. The cons she had designed back when she was a teenager were still being used long after she had left the life behind.

Auntie Tiff had committed the ultimate sin.

She had married a cop and committed to living by society's rules.

I can't even remember ever having met her, even if Piper insists we did. When Tiff passed away, she left her home to the two of us.

We finally had something that was our very own, well, I did. Piper had her degree by then, because why do something in four years if you can do it in under three? She had been hired on as a consultant, which sounded like a con in and of itself to me, but the fancy firm let her work from wherever she wanted.

TIN

I'd never thought I'd be living in the panhandle of Oklahoma, but the price was right and it was far enough away from our family that I was able to piece together a bit of my own life. We slowly started to fix the house up and I did my best to ignore my mother and aunts. Until they sent our uncle around.

From the time I had moved into our inherited house with Piper, then started writing my books, our dear family kept a ledger on their losses from what I had been earning for them. When I told my uncle that I was out, he smirked at me and threw out the number they figured they deserved from the two of us.

There was no fucking way I was going to let them near her, she'd made her break and was doing really well. I told them I'd do two jobs a year for three years then if I ever heard from them again, I'd email a file I had on them with all the jobs they had done to the feds.

Sometimes it pays to be known as the *crazy* one.

The problem was, I found out I wasn't as smart as I thought. My family decided to set me up, blackmail Piper, and make off with the box I have in my backpack.

TWO

Tin

I can't remember the last time I've enjoyed myself so much.

Paige keeps expecting me to do what she wants every time she opens her mouth, to the point that I'm fairly certain she's been manipulating men since her big brown eyes took their first peek at the world around her, but I ain't falling for that shit.

From what Parker has relayed to me, I know that Piper is estranged from the rest of their family and all he would say on that subject was that it was for the best. But I didn't miss the new motion detectors and extra cameras he set up on his land and around the clubhouse.

He'll tell me what I need to know if he gets wind

of anything solid, but in the meantime, his actions tell me that Piper, and therefore Paige, might be in some degree of danger, herself.

"Shit," I mumble to myself, recalling our earlier conversation.

Reaching for my phone, I dial Parker's number.

"All good?" he asks by way of a greeting.

"All good," I tell him. "Look, I mentioned Piper's pregnancy and Paige didn't know about it. I wanted to give you two a heads up so no one's blindsided."

"What's your read on her?" Parker's next question momentarily takes me by surprise, wondering if he's gleaned enough to know that she and his Ol' Lady are very different people.

"She's ugly as sin," I respond, buying myself a minute.

"We've already established they're identical, you motherfucker," he grunts.

"So, if I see her naked, it'll count as seeing Piper naked?" I barely have that gem out of my mouth when he's diving into his Cornish past to cuss me out six ways to Sunday. Mission accomplished, I think as I wait for him to simmer down.

"Well, then, rest assured. You got the good twin, this is the bad one." I grin as I tell him that, thinking about how flustered Piper gets when she's put on the spot and doesn't want to lie or hurt someone's feelings.

"Even if she's a pain, get her back here safe and sound." I can hear something close to relief in his voice and know that some part of him will always be wary after what he went through with his ex. "No fucking around with her."

"Would I do that?" I shoot back, failing miserably at my attempt to sound innocent.

"Bastard."

With that, he disconnects the phone and while the idea of taking Paige for a test drive is more than appealing, I can see where it might get dicey since she's Piper's family and will undoubtedly be around.

When I emerge from my room, I find Paige fiddling with the washer, having changed into a skirt that's barely longer than the shorts she had been wearing along with a tank top.

"I need to go to the store tomorrow, can you drop me off when you head to your meeting?" Her question acknowledges my presence, but she doesn't bother to look back at me.

"No, you'll stay here. We can stop along the way home," I tell her. "You ready to go?"

"Yep," she says, drawing out the 'P' as much as possible.

"Are you really a vegetarian?"

"Nope." There she goes popping that 'P' again. I almost say something, before considering her lack of eye contact and wonder if she got ahold of her sister while I was in my room.

Shaking my head, I have to remind myself not to get involved in this woman's emotional quagmire. Instead, I turn on my heel and circle my finger in the air, guessing she's clever enough to follow me out to the truck.

I'm pulling my seatbelt across my chest when I realize I'd forgotten to lock up and appreciate the fact that she's doing it for me.

"Don't tell me y'all live somewhere you don't lock the doors?" And, *she's back*. I pull out and start navigating traffic without a word, until she prompts me, "Well?"

"You said not to tell you," I answer her, unable to keep the smile out of my voice.

"Seriously? You don't lock the door to your house when you leave? You just leave it unlocked for anyone to wander in?" Paige sounds truly outraged at the concept.

"I suppose if they wanted in, they could just climb through the open window," I answer with a shrug, wondering how far down the path she'll follow my bullshit.

"And at night? What about when you're sleeping? Anyone could get in and kill you! Tell me that Me'ansome locks his fucking doors!" Paige's voice is approaching the 'nails on a chalkboard' level of hysteria when I finally cast a smirk in her direction and get punched in the shoulder for my effort. "You are such a dick!"

"That makes it sound like I'm growing on ya," I drawl out. "It sounds considerably better than, what did you call me earlier? An asshole?"

"I've been meaning to ask you, what's Me'ansome's actual name? I feel weird calling him that," Paige asks, her voice sweet as can be—giving me whiplash with her sudden change.

"Parker," I answer, not worrying about giving up his name since most of the men call him that anyway.

"Parker and Piper," she whispers more to herself than to me.

"I thought you would have talked to your sister already?" At this stage, their dynamic has me baffled.

"We talked, but we don't say names or specifics over the phone," she tells me and I weigh her words while turning into the parking lot.

Who the fuck are these girls? I wonder as we're

being seated and I immediately place our drink order with the hostess.

"How exactly do you two exchange information if you don't talk about specifics?" I ask, leaning across the table and brushing a strand of her long, dark purple hair off of her cheek.

That simple movement startles us both, but for the first time, she doesn't shield her response from me and her eyes soften.

"We worked out a system when we were kids," Paige tells me as our waiter plops our drinks down. Once he has our order, I get more insight into the twins. "The basic premise remains the same, but we update the things that we reference to get our message across."

"You started doing this as kids?" I prompt her for more of the story and her shield drops back down into place before she leans across the table, distracting me with her cleavage.

"We were raised by wolves," she whispers, her voice deadly serious even as I see the humor in her eyes.

I shake my head, keeping my gaze on hers. "Wolves are fiercely devoted to their families. Hyenas, those are the bitches that'll kill the young in their pack to show their dominance."

"Seriously?" she asks, looking annoyed. "I've been fucking up that awesome line for years?"

"Sorry, kid." I'm not and she knows it as we both throw back our drinks. "Another?"

Paige nods and winks in the direction of the waiter to get his attention, before circling her finger over the tops of our empty glasses.

"Keep them coming," I tell him when he delivers them and asks if she needs anything else.

The next hour flies by and Paige finally lets out a sigh as she finishes her T-bone steak and I'm trying to figure out how she managed to eat it all as she's slimmer than Piper was before her pregnancy.

When we move from the table to sit at the bar, she gets handsier with me and while I'm enjoying the fuck out of the attention, I won't be taking advantage of the situation tonight.

Paige

This man is a goddamn vault. Cold, hard steel.

Tin probably thinks he's getting me tipsy, but I'm barely buzzed; I'm just acting like a nearly drunk, sorority girl to soften him up and get him talking, but he refuses to give me any decent information on Parker and Piper. The ass even shifted away from me the last time I ran my hand up his arm.

"How old are you?" I blurt the question out and cringe at how sober I sound, unlike how I've been speaking the past thirty or so minutes.

"Old enough to know it's a good time to close out the tab," he responds, and flags down the bartender.

"Oh, that's no fun! Look the band is setting up," I tell him. Well, maybe I'm a little buzzed.

"One of us has to work tomorrow and the other one has to be a good girl and do what she's told."

I must admit, I like the look he gives me whenever he says shit to get a rise out of me; in this case, his eyes hold a promise of what he likes to do to *bad* girls.

"I'm very good at a lot of things," I tell him, leaning forward to brush my breast against his arm just as the bartender returns with the check, giving

Tin such an obvious grin, he might as well have just high-fived him for having me on his arm.

Once again, Tin pulls out some bills and tosses them down, seemingly without counting, but I know he's smarter than that and it occurs to me that I'm playing him all wrong.

Biker or not, he's also a lawyer who can practice in several states. He must have mentally tallied the cost of the meal, then later the bar tab plus the tip. He barely glanced at the check either time, so he must have just been verifying it before paying.

He's smart. He said earlier he has no problem getting women and as handsome as he is, I can more than understand that. From the first look Tin gave me, I knew he viewed me as *trouble*, most men do try to play up to that persona, figuring they'll have a few good times with me before they move along.

Tin is on this trip to do a job and isn't looking for a distraction.

"You look like you solved the Riddle of the Sphinx," Tin says when we're nearly to his truck.

"That would only be helpful if I could solve the second riddle, also," I immediately reply, keeping a straight face when I see a flicker of surprise light up his eyes.

"Not many people know that there were two questions," he murmurs, opening my door for me.

"The Sphinx wasn't very big on leaving witnesses, now was she?" I toss out when he gets in on his side.

"No, a bit of a man-eater, that one," he replies, his expression telling me he considers me to be in the same category. "What made you start writing romance?"

"Why do you ask?"

"I would have pegged you for more of the espionage or complicated heist type," he answers after a moment.

"Well, that hits too close to home, so I decided to write about something I know nothing about."

"Sex?" he bites out with a laugh.

"Oh! And he's a tiny bit funny when he's not being an asshole," I concede, unable to keep my own laughter in. "Happily ever after, was what I actually meant."

"You don't think it's possible?"

"Do you?" I counter his question, suddenly curious about his take on it.

"Fuck no." That answer bursts from him before he looks more thoughtful. "That's how I always felt about it, but now, there are some people that I care for and I really hope I'm wrong about it."

His blunt, honest answer is a thousand degrees different from anything I expected him to say and leaves me speechless. And if I were the type of girl to swoon, I might even be inclined to do so.

"By some people, do you mean Parker and Piper?" I finally ask when he's unlocking the door to the rental house.

"Yeah, them. And Joey."

"Who's Joey?" I ask, crossing to grab a couple of bottles of water from the fridge and move toward the couch. He looks like he's going to ignore me for a moment, but something in his countenance shifts and he crosses the room to take one from my outstretched hand before sitting on the ottoman in front of the fireplace.

"She's Parker's daughter," he replies after a moment, and I know it's because he's weighing how much to tell me. "Joey was raised by her mother's family, Christ, that bitch is a piece of work. After Joey graduated from high school she came looking for her dad, but she met Axel first and they had a very unconventional and whirlwind courtship."

"And do you like Axel?"

"He's a berserker," Tin says by way of an answer, and I know surprise flashes clearly across my face. "He's this monstrously huge guy and used to fight in this underground ring. Those fights are like nothing you could imagine."

Tin tips his head as almost an apology to me

when I raise an eyebrow at him. I have actually been to underground fights as my family considered them great crowds to practice pickpocketing on.

"I'd want him on my side in a fight, that's for certain, but married to Parker's daughter…" he cuts off his sentence with a shrug of his shoulders. "They somehow seem right together though, and I wouldn't want her to go through the pain of a breakup."

"Is he in your MC?"

"No, he's a Royal Bastard," Tin replies, standing up and stretching his back. I nod my head, familiar enough with the name as they're a fairly large, nationwide MC. "I'm going to turn in. I'll wake you before I leave in the morning."

"There's a Red Circle store nearby, I need some things before you leave for the day," I inform him, deciding to play it straight. "Namely food and clean underwear. Unless you want me ordering delivery or making friends with the neighbors?"

"We'll be there when the doors open and you'll have twenty minutes, in and out," Tin concedes, and I feel like I've won a major battle. "Be ready to tell me about that item you swiped on the way to the store in the morning. I need to know in case there's trouble."

His parting line steals my brief victory and I nearly growl in frustration.

I'm utterly exhausted the next morning and doubt I would have pulled myself out of bed if not for the smell of coffee.

Tin looks at me and grunts when I show my face a few minutes later. A very large part of me is relieved he's about as much of a morning person as I am. Once we both finish our coffees, we head out to his truck in companionable silence and he sets up the GPS to get us to the store.

"Do you want anything?" I ask, I notice he's going to stay in the truck while I head inside.

"I want you back here in twenty minutes and you can tell me whatever story you rehearsed all last night." With that, he moves his seat back and closes his eyes.

I try really hard not to slam the truck door behind me. I failed, but I didn't bother looking back; mostly because I was certain that shit-eating grin of his would be pointed in my direction. When I returned, twenty-three minutes later, I loaded up the back seat with my finds and got in without saying a word.

If he was already insinuating that I had spent last

night making up a story, he wasn't going to believe the tale I had crafted during our drive the afternoon before. There was no point in letting him shoot holes in it and use it to doubt anything I said in the future.

Neither one of us say a word during the short trip back to the rental and I wave him off when he asks me if I need help with the bags. With multiple bags hanging off both arms, I make it up to the porch and unlock the door with the key I had kept this morning —because as soon as I sort through everything and eat breakfast, I am heading over to that pool.

THREE

Paige

Tin returns when I'm almost done cooking dinner and he looks exhausted. He simply pats me on my back before accepting the plate I dish up for him and he gets himself a glass of water, before taking them both to his room and not emerging for several more hours.

"Is there any more of that dinner?" he asks, looking discouraged when he sees that the kitchen has been thoroughly cleaned.

"There's some in the fridge. I also made sandwiches for the road and have some other snacks, we'll have to buy drinks along the way," I tell him and get an appreciative nod from him.

Apparently, my evil plan of acting like a responsible adult is working.

Before long, we pack up the rest of our things and return the key to the lockbox as we head out on the next segment of our journey.

"So, how was your day today, dear?" I ask him, more than a little curious to find out what he was up to.

He chuckles, shaking his head without saying anything.

"My day was leisurely." I decide to talk his ear off once I realize he's not going to talk. "I went to the pool and worked on my tan. But it was a scorcher today, so I blasted the air conditioner and got some words in."

"Words in?" he asks, confusion clouding his face for a moment.

"I try to keep track of how much I write every day. Ideally, I'd be doing a certain amount per day, but I've been on the fly recently so now I'm just squeezing them in when I can."

"Joey started reading your books after meeting your sister, she really seems to like them," Tin offers in response.

"Piper's been so great, handling my advertising and social media and all. I had no clue what I was getting myself into when I started self-publishing," I tell him, hugging my arms across my chest.

"You cold?"

"What? Oh, no, just kind of missing Piper. Do you have any siblings?"

"I have a brother," he answers me without further explanation.

"Is he in the same MC as you?"

"No, he's in the Royal Bastards with Axel."

"Hmm," I answer and bite my tongue on the six million questions I have for him, knowing that the more I ask him, the quicker he'll get around to asking about the contents of my backpack.

"Just so you know, I typically stop for twenty minutes every three hours and stop to sleep every fourteen hours, but this route will throw that pattern off…"

"You got some military precision thing going there, don't you?" My rhetorical question leaves him looking less than impressed so I decide to kick it up a notch. "I've never had sex with a man your age. Maybe we can stop closer to the ten-hour mark and take care of that?"

"Why? I have that factored into all of the twenty-minute breaks," he instantly shoots back at me, and I laugh, impressed not just by his wit, but the perplexed look he takes on for his delivery, barely catching his mumbled, 'Man my age'.

We're about two hours into the trip when I notice the four-door, black Cadillac keeping a steady pace behind us and I slide down a little further along the seat.

"You alright?" Tin asks, paying more attention to me than the road.

"Yep."

"Anything you want to tell me about the guys on our tail?" he nonchalantly asks as he changes lanes.

"What are you talking about?" I question him, looking confused before throwing a glance over my shoulder and hoping he doesn't notice that I'm using the headrest to conceal my face.

"You're a better liar than your sister, but let me assure you, the kind of people who follow me would be on motorcycles, not a late model Cadillac."

"Honestly, if Me'ansome is anything like you, I have no idea what she's gotten herself into, but I'll be sure to get her out of it," I assure him, while I try to figure out how to get us out of this situation.

"If I thought you had a chance of doing that, I'd pull over and hand you over to those two idiots back there." His voice is deeper and slightly terrifying, causing my jaw to drop open as I turn to look at him. "Time to start talking."

"Are they happy?" I'm not even stalling for time with that question. I don't know much about the man next to me, but his threat left zero doubt about his belief in them as a couple.

"Yes."

"You mentioned he has a daughter, does he have any other children?"

"Me'ansome has twenty-one-year-old twins," he tells me with a sigh, figuring out that I'm not sharing anything until I get the information he's been withholding. "It's Joey who was supposed to attend that signing. She jacked up her ankle and knee, making the trip impossible, so Parker picked up the books she wanted and met your sister there. Then there's Ransom, he'll lead the Knights someday. He's a good fucking kid."

"Fuck," I mumble under my breath.

Parker's kids are literally our age! I wonder how that's going over with everyone.

"Are you two the same age?" I ask and he shrugs. "How do you not know that?"

"I guess we're close in age, but it's not like we ever sat around discussing what fucking moon we were born under," he chuckles and screws up his face like I'm the crazy one.

"How long have you known him?"

"Hmm. Since before his ex, but less than thirty

years, I guess." His answer drives home the point that he and Me'ansome have been friends longer than Piper and I have been alive.

"And you two are close?"

"I consider him my brother and I helped him raise his son," Tin replies. "Just so you know, I'm tallying up all these questions and I expect you to, *honestly*, answer the same amount. You're at five."

"You said you helped him raise his son, not both of them?"

"Joey's mother—took her when she left for good. Joey came and found us a few years ago." There's a story there, I can tell by what he didn't say, but that's not important right now.

"You said he's your brother, how does your actual brother feel about that?"

"Red and I are blood, but we chose different routes. I've lied and kept things from him over the years in the name of the Knights or for Parker. And from the time the twins were born, helping Parker protect and care for them became our priority."

While the fact that Me'ansome's children are basically the same age as Piper and me was the most startling information I learned today, the most interesting was Tin using the words 'us' and 'ours' just now.

He truly considers Me'ansome, Ransom, and Joey to be his family.

If that's the case, maybe he'll be as protective of Piper and her child, wait! Twins. Lots of fucking twins in this equation.

"Does Piper know the sex of her children yet?" I ask, reaching across to grasp his bicep. Shit, that makes seven questions, I think, before I'm distracted by him flexing his arm.

"Me'ansome didn't mention it, if they did. He was too busy freaking out about another set of twins." His answer none-to-subtly corrects the wording of my question, but answers the question I didn't ask. Those babies will be well looked after.

"Yeah, now considering what the four of you are named, I'm going to need you to help me make sure they don't go crazy over names starting with 'P'," Tin tells me that like it's the biggest problem we have right now.

"The four of us?" I ask, confused about the fourth person.

"Parker had a twin brother. Parson."

I miss neither the past tense, nor the timber of Tin's voice in his brief explanation. Parson's dead and it was apparently not a *loss* by Tin's account.

I decide that's irrelevant right now as I throw

another look over my shoulder. "More importantly, what about our tail?"

"There are too many cars on the road right now for them to try anything, plus there's a state trooper four vehicles up from us," he answers me and I lean forward, not having noticed any cops in the area. "Now, why don't you tell me what you stole the other day?"

"Y'know, it's pretty rude to assume something like that." My glare has no effect on Tin, whatsoever. Dammit, it's probably because he met Piper first and she's, well, I guess, she's like the sweet to my sour.

I turn to look out of the window and wait for him to say something else, but he doesn't bite, he's seemingly content to drive without talking. I reach over to turn on the radio, but as soon as I settle back into my seat, he drops the volume to that really annoyingly, low level—where you can barely hear the sound, but know that it's there anyway.

"Look," I finally say, not being able to stand the silence anymore. "It was my great-grandmother's broach. A cousin of mine lost it in a poker game and I tracked it down."

"Uh-huh," he grunts, looking skeptical, but letting the silence fall between us again.

"I'm serious. She's dead and it's not even that valuable, other than for sentimental reasons," I blurt out without thinking, and almost instantly cringe knowing how dumb that sounds. "It belongs in my family."

"Who owned that pawn shop?" he asks after a moment and I've got to hand it to him, he hit the nail on the head with that question. "And remember, I answered all of your questions *honestly*."

"A cousin, of sorts," I mumble and get a snort from him. "I didn't know him, it's like a second or third cousin once or twice removed, or some nonsense like that."

"Who happens to be a descendent of the same great-grandmother?"

"One of her sisters' descendants, yes."

Tin

Well, she isn't fucking boring.

The glimpses I have had of who Paige, when she's not playing up one of the many personas I'm sure she had to adopt over the years, is downright endearing.

Her sister has the drive of an A-type personality, but she authentically cares about people and puts those around her at ease, versus Paige's soft side which resembles a cactus.

That doesn't bother me though. My road name is the short version of The Tin Man and the only difference between me and the character from The Wizard of Oz is that I never gave a shit about being heartless.

Or unfeeling, cold, callus, or whatever synonyms were thrown my way. Whether it was by my family or any number of women I fucked over the years.

I'm sure I cried when I was a kid, but I only really remember crying when my older brother came to tell me he was leaving and never coming back. The last beating from our old man had been too much for him, and Mom, who was typically strung out on something, never gave a shit.

I begged Red to take me with him, but he didn't know how he was going to take care of himself, let alone a nine-year-old. And like everyone else, once he left, he never looked back.

It was nearly twenty years before our paths crossed again. We were at the rally up in South Dakota, Red was a Royal Bastard and Parker and I, had been riding as Grave Knights for some time.

I never once considered looking for him and had expected the same from him, so I was momentarily annoyed when a Bastard interrupted me and the girls I was hoping to entertain in my tent later that night. He had put his hand on my shoulder and looked into my eyes before clasping me in a tight embrace.

"Brother," he rasped out, his voice thick with emotion and alcohol, as I was trying to figure out who he was, the only emotion I had was frustration as the women had melted back into the crowd. I knew there would be others, but I had invested a bit of time in warming those two up.

"I ain't your fucking brother," I spit back, glancing down at his cut long enough to get an idea of how his life had been spent in the years since he left me to fend for myself.

The biggest surprise being, that even though we hailed from Maine, we lived within an easy ride of each other. Him in Arizona and me in Utah, but there was more than a state border that separated us and while Red is as easy-going as they come, I've kept him at arm's length since then.

Except when Parker asked me to reach out, to help grow our business. And that made sense, so I had no issue with it. But over the years, Red would ask questions about rumors he had heard about Ransom having a sister and other things old ladies like to gossip about. I always played dumb, either shrugging them off or giving a half truth.

Because as I learned in law school, in those matters: one question satisfactorily answered, generally leads to another question. 'Answer the first question at the peril of finding out what the next question is', at least, that's how one of the professors phrased it.

I never considered it a betrayal because, even though he's not blood related, Parker King is my brother in every way that counts.

Besides saving my life a time or two, while I was content to ride on the weekends with some buddies, he was the one who decided to form our own MC. The time I got obliterated and mentioned that I'd make a righteous fucking lawyer, he filed that away and chased down a huge score—solely to be able to give me the money to pay for college and law school.

When I warned him that Jayne was no good and that running off to Vegas was the stupidest thing I'd ever heard of, he still insisted that I should be there by his side that night.

And when their children were born, I stood by him, proud as hell to be Tommy and Joey's godfather even as his relationship with Jayne was imploding. But it was the day he handed his infant son to me, asking me to hide him and keep him away from her family until he got the MC in order—that I knew that Parker considered me every bit his brother.

I was thrown for a loop when Joey came back into our lives and I smother a grin at the memory of Axel nearly losing his shit when he saw Ransom flirting with his Ol' Lady, who was nothing more than a stranger at a gas station to us. Later that week, when I pieced together who she was, I thought everything would change.

And they did—for the better.

In many ways, Joey is more like Parker than Ransom is—with her strength and loyalty being some of her best qualities. In that moment, it strikes me that without Joey in our lives, Parker wouldn't have met Piper.

And with no Piper in our world, I wouldn't be sitting here next to Paige. But only time will tell how this is going to end. I glance over at her thighs again before shifting in my seat, my dick twitching in response to the thought of exploring her body.

"We're coming up on one of your scheduled stops," Paige says, breaking into my thoughts.

"I was hoping to see the trooper pull off and stop where he does. Are you armed by any chance?" I ask, only having my Sig with me, but know that I could get one of the guys from Reno's Battle Born MC to meet me with a couple of guns and more ammo if I think we're going to need it.

"No, I mean, just a knife and some pepper spray," she answers me, shrugging like everyone walks around with those items, at a bare minimum. "My Glock's in my car back in Vegas."

"Can I assume that's where your family is waiting for you?"

"Some of them, yes. Most of them will be back in Louisiana this time of year," she sighs. "I am fucked if they find my car."

"Where is it?"

"I left the decoy…"

"Decoy?" I ask, needing her to rewind her story.

"I have a Hellcat, in granite. It makes an impression," she answers with a proud grin.

"Redeye or Widebody?"

"Redeye. Of course, but since I couldn't find one of those to rent I had to go with the standard Hellcat. Since we're on the subject, mind me asking what you usually ride?"

"Now, my baby is a thing of beauty. Not that having a truck doesn't come in handy," I tell Paige, caressing the steering wheel so my Denali doesn't get jealous. "I have a Harley Street Glide, with a twenty-six inch front wheel all blacked out, and sixteen inch apes."

"What are apes?" she asks and I groan.

"You literally write about motorcycle clubs," I point out, more than a little exasperated.

"Yes, but in an 'Oh, look at that. That's pretty.' kind of way." She shrugs back at me.

"Apes are the handlebars."

"Yes, I worked that out while I was soaking in your disappointment, thank you," she sasses back, crossing her arms over her chest before suddenly pointing up ahead of us. "Hey! The cop is pulling off."

Nodding to indicate that I see the trooper shifting onto the exit ramp, I take it slow and smile when the Cadillac makes its move to pull up alongside us. Waiting until the last second, I swerve off of the highway, leaving them no chance but to ride onto the next exit. Unless they find an emergency turnaround, of course.

Approaching the end of the ramp, I turn off my lights to make it more difficult for them to see which way we're heading.

"Pull up your map app. Get me side roads heading north or east and hopefully one with an all-night gas station along the way," I snap off directions to Paige and am relieved she does what I ask without question.

"That was Felix in the passenger seat," Paige says after we have our new route set up.

"Great. I've heard all about your cousin," I let her know and enjoy the momentary surprise on her face.

"Piper doesn't know the half of it."

"No, but Tober does."

"What! How did you and Tober meet?" she asks, not even attempting to play it cool.

"You really need to pick up the phone and have an actual conversation with your sister," I groan out. "They kidnapped her."

"What?" Her shout blows out my ear drum as she grabs my wrist.

"Well, she likes to say they baby-knapped her, because it was less than a day." I shake my head, knowing I sound ridiculous repeating the nonsensical phrase that Piper coined, but it gets a laugh from her sister beside me.

"That sounds like Piper, all right. Please tell me what happened."

Exactly to Piper's point, it's a short story so I quickly get Paige up to speed before I continue, "So, I brought the Caddy to a chop shop I know, then attached the tracker they found to a big rig to send Felix on a little chase. Meanwhile, Tober went and stayed at Parker's house for a couple of weeks and that's when we sat him down to try to get the lay of the land. He found some ranch to work on in Oregon and seems to be doing alright."

"They never should have involved Tober," Paige's

stern voice indicates how strong her feelings are on that matter.

"I can't say I disagree." I carefully find the best way to express my opinion about the large guy who is about eighty percent heart and twenty percent brain function. "But if he wasn't assigned to be Felix's driver, then I don't know where Piper would be now."

Paige lets out a sigh, conceding to my point; her grip on my arm loosens, but she doesn't seem to be in any hurry to retract her hand.

"They're slipping," Paige says in a near whisper.

"What do you mean?"

"Piper was always good to Tober and while he forgets most of the basics, he wouldn't have been likely to ever forget her kindness," she elaborates and I nod, understanding that he didn't have many people who were good to him.

Taken in that light, she's right. That should have been considered when sending people out to pick up Piper.

We spend the next thirty miles crisscrossing backroads and dodging the wildlife who reclaim these roads as theirs once the sun goes down.

"Stop doing that!" Even to my own ears, I sound like I'm strangling as I plead with Paige to stop pumping her imaginary break. "I have nearly perfect vision."

"Yeah, well, it's the *nearly* I'm worried about. Why won't you let me drive?"

I should have kept my mouth shut, I think as I tighten my fingers around the steering wheel, while I picture her tan skin in my hands.

Just as she opens her mouth, we both catch sight of lights in the distance and breathe a sigh of relief. It has to be the gas station and diner she's been insisting was still ahead of us—each time her phone caught a signal.

The smell of the fresh-baked pie hits me as soon as we enter and fuck our schedule, I'm suddenly determined that we're going to sit down to eat.

"Can you get me a coffee? I'm going to the bathroom," Paige says heading off to the back of the diner without waiting for an answer.

"Sit at the counter if you're eating in!" A man calls out from the window to the kitchen and I walk to the only space there are two seats together, nodding at the guy in the seat next to the one I take.

I look at the menu while I wait on both service and Paige; turns out the former was delayed by the latter, as they exit the bathroom laughing like they're old friends.

Paige's dark eyes scan the room, looking slightly surprised to see that I've settled in to eat here, but she acknowledges me with the tilt of her head and the waitress leans in to say something that has them both laughing—drawing the attention of every man at the counter.

Sitting next to me, she leans in like she's going to kiss my cheek, but whispers, "Play along."

"Here you go, sweetie," the waitress says, coming straight over with two cups of coffee before going down the line and refilling everyone's mug and brewing a fresh pot.

"Now what'll you have?"

"What kind of pie is that I'm smelling?"

"Peach and the best you'll have anywhere," she assures me with a wink.

Turning to look at Paige, I give her my widest grin. "Don't you know? I just love fresh, peach pie."

The man to my right snorts in amusement and the waitress who looks like she has a couple of years on me gives me another wink for my effort.

"I'd be willing to give you all the peach pie you could stand, but I think your girl here would scratch my eyes out." The waitress leans in, her elbows on the counter giving me a pretty clear view of her impressive cleavage and I feel Paige press up against my side.

"I've been coming here for twenty years," the man to my right speaks up, his head practically on my shoulder as he enjoys the view. "You never offered me any of your pie."

"What? And lose out on twenty years' worth of tips from you, Marv?" she counters, before looking over at Paige. "What can I get for you, hun?"

"Just a side salad with French dressing," Paige responds and I look down at her like she's lost her mind.

"There's just no accounting for taste, now is there?" I ask her.

"Obviously not," retorts the younger man sitting on the far side of Paige as his eyes travel up her body until they get to me, glaring at him over her head.

With that, I wrap my arm around her waist and take a sip of the surprisingly decent coffee. I barely notice the waitress coming back toward us until the man to my right starts to laugh, then I look up to see it.

"Side salad, French dressing," she says, putting a basket of fries in front of Paige before she grabs a bottle of ketchup from her apron to complete that order. "And here's your *fresh*, peach pie."

My pie is served with another wink as I laugh

with the others and she makes another round with the coffee pot.

"Well played, Paige. Well played," I compliment the woman beside me, kissing her temple without thinking. I'm just too busy trying to figure out how she and the waitress bonded in the bathroom so damn quick.

FOUR

Paige

"Tin?" I quietly call his name, knocking on the connecting door even as I'm pushing it open. "Yeah?"

"Can I sleep in here with you tonight?" I ask, hugging my arms across my chest as he frowns at me. "I don't snore."

Without a word, he nods his head as he indicates the far side of the bed and I instinctively know he wants to stay between me and the main door. I circle around it, not wanting to push my luck by saying anything and crawl under the covers, scootching over to the middle.

He rolls onto his left side to face me, not saying a word as I get comfortable.

"Thank you," I whisper, feeling the need to say something. We're lying about a foot away from each other and in typical Tin fashion, I think he could go on looking at me until I fall asleep. Just calmly watching and studying me, making me nervous wondering what it is he sees when he looks at me.

"Paige, when Piper left for college, why didn't you go with her?" he asks a few moments after I had given up hope of him speaking.

"Because my family was all I knew and I enjoyed the work. Getting the better of the marks, out-smarting all of those people who just thought I was a pretty face—that's a huge rush when you're a kid," I add for good measure and hear him let out a soft scoff.

"Paige?" he says my name in question and I raise an eyebrow in response. "Why didn't you go with Piper when she made a break for it?"

The shrewd look he's leveling at me, as he rephrases his original question makes it hard not to squirm, but I refuse to break eye contact with him.

"You didn't leave because they would have gone after you both and destroyed her dream. You sacrificed yourself, because you knew that Piper wouldn't have lasted a year leading that life. And the moment she got caught, your family would have killed her, correct?"

TIN

Tears are streaming down my face and I stare into the eyes of the only man who has ever seen me clearly and I want to curse the gods for putting him in my path before I could break away from my family and become the person that Piper has always believed I could be.

"Does she know what you did for her?"

"It wasn't just for her," I tell him when I'm able to speak. "When *they* decide someone needs to be cut loose, they send the person closest to them to carry out the kill. Piper doesn't know it, but it was our mother who killed our father."

"And this job? They told you it would be your last one, didn't they?"

"That isn't why I went through with it," I let him know, unable to stop the smile that flits across my face. "I mean, the whole thing was an obvious set up from the start. It's just that I can use the ugly fucking thing to destroy my family."

"What do you mean?"

"Our great-grandmother was one of four sisters who came to the U.S. sometime in the early 1900s; Piper is better with the dates and whole family tree thing than I am. Anyway, each of the sisters had a piece of jewelry that their father had given them. He was like the rest of us, a thief and a confidence man except, not having a son, he set up this whole

57

competitive thing among them that's still in play today."

"Like Olympics for criminals?" Tin cracks that gem and I nod, squirming a little closer to him before I continue the story.

"Every few years, they get together—under their crest, which is the jewelry from our great-great grandfather—and compare the jobs they accomplished. Whichever family's accomplishments have the highest monetary value, the others have to give them twenty percent of the value they had come to the table with." I pause for a moment, repeatedly swallowing to relieve my dry throat, and Tin gets up to grab a bottle of water from his cooler.

He twists the cap off before getting into bed and I appreciate the fact that I probably would have spilled the water over myself wrestling with the safety seal. I don't miss that he settles even closer to me than we were before.

"So, the four families are meeting soon?" he asks to prompt me along after I've had a few sips.

"No, there are only three now. Our great-aunt, she fell in love with a federal marshal and surrendered the ruby she had been given. I think she saw something in Piper and me when we were young because when Aunt Tiff died, she left her house to us."

TIN

"Just to Piper," Tin interrupts me and my eyes widen in disbelief. "She had me review some documents since she wants to sell the house."

"Piper said it was for both of us." I can't help the sniffle I let out and know that in her heart, she did it to help me start to break away from our mother and her siblings.

"And what happens if your family doesn't have the broach when the meeting comes around?"

"If a member of one of the other families has it, they can lay claim to all of our earnings from the last couple of years—whether in assets or forcing them to pull off jobs for them—until they're able to reclaim it. If it is forfeited or lost, then our family's seat is dissolved permanently. My cousins can request to work for one of the other branches, but it depends on their level of skill, if they'll be accepted."

"What are you going to do with it?"

"Believe me when I tell you, that seat means everything to my family. They're so fucking obsessed with it." I stop and take a breath, trying to push down the anger I've carried for so long. "They've taken so much from us. I won't let them have it."

With that, Tin's lips press against mine and the searing heat of my rage instantly transforms into need. I've spent half of the last few days ready to strangle this man, but his cool head and warm heart call to me as no other has and my body quickly responds to him.

Reaching down, my fingers search for the hem of my nightshirt and I lift it up, tossing it to the side as he groans and buries his head into my neck, nibbling along my collarbone.

My fingers dance over the landscape of Tin's body, learning his hidden scars as he leans down to take one of my nipples into his mouth and roll it between his tongue and lips. Leaving chilly, hardened peaks in his path as he shifts to different areas until finally rolling onto his back.

I lie on my side, my head propped up with one hand as my other one lazily wanders down my side, eventually running into the edge of my panties. I smile, enjoying how Tin's eyes have followed the trail even as he removes his boxers and reaches for his wallet behind him.

Hopefully, between the condom he retrieves and the birth control that I'm on, we won't find ourselves caring for a child anytime soon.

I start to remove my panties, but he shakes his head, "Leave them on."

It's his turn to smile when I slide up over him, shifting the scrap of lace to the side as I line his cock up with my sheath and slowly make my way down his length.

TIN

"Fuck yeah," he grunts out when I tighten my muscles around him, lacing his fingers behind his head shows me that he's letting me take the wheel for the first time since we've been together.

I swivel my hips, getting used to the feel of his thick cock inside of me and reach out, bracing myself on the wall above his head—gasping when Tin leans up to lick at my nipples.

Leaning forward, I hook my feet back over his thighs to give myself the leverage I enjoy and slowly start to ride him, adjusting my hips until I get his cock to hit my sweet spot every time I lower myself. Getting into a satisfying rhythm, I shift my feet off his legs and lean backward, as his knees raise up so I can grasp them.

As I feel the tingles start in my toes and pleasure from every nerve ending, I start to move faster and faster, almost clumsily in my eagerness and that's when I feel his fingers squeezing into my hips, as though putting the brakes on.

"No, what are you doing?" The words come out in a whine as he slows my approach to the peak I was so close to.

It's quickly obvious that his age has its advantages. Unlike men my age who would just plow into me and enjoy the sight of my breasts bouncing, when he takes over, he adjusts his angle with each thrust. Rolling his hips and grinding against me as he slowly pulls out before penetrating me again and again.

Even though he took over our rhythm, I never once felt that his focus was anywhere but on my needs.

Looking down into his eyes, it took me a moment to place the emotion I saw there. The word 'possessiveness' clicked in my mind and that, almost more than the physical act we were playing out, pushed my body over the crest I hadn't been able to reach on my own.

Tin's hands tighten on my hips and he rolls me onto my back, continuing to pump into me until his strangled cry tells me when he finds his release. Collapsing on top of me, he supports most of his weight on his elbows; his sweat drips from his forehead, mingling with mine as we both strive to regulate our breathing.

Tapping his shoulder, I roll out from underneath him and head to the bathroom to get cleaned up. While in there, I stall a bit longer than I should, wondering if I it's best to head back to my room or crawl into bed with him.

A sharp rap on the door interrupts my indecision and I open it to see Tin gripping either side of the door frame, blocking my exit.

"Don't want you getting any ideas about sleeping in your room tonight," he says, stepping aside to effectively block the open door between our rooms, and leaving a clear path to his bed.

"Um, can I just grab the comforter from my bed?" I ask him and although he raises an eyebrow at my requests he turns to go get it for me.

I craw into his bed and wait for him to come back, smiling when he unfurls the blanket into the air, letting it drift down over my body. My need for the second cover becomes immediately clear to him when I instantly burrito myself in it.

He gives me a goofy grin, shaking his head as he crawls in next to me and stretches an arm until I scootch into his side. "I feel like this is the modern version of how the couples on *I Love Lucy* slept."

"Am I supposed to know what that is?" I ask, seeing if he'll take the bait.

"Shut up and go to sleep," he grumbles back to me.

And hours later, when I wake to his lips on my neck, I realize it was the most restful sleep I've had in a very long time.

"What are you doing?" I grumble as he untucks my blanket, letting a draft into my perfect cocoon.

"Warming you up." His lips vibrate against my stomach as he kisses his way down my body.

Spreading my legs, he slides his body between them as he leans in, swirling his tongue around my clit. I can't stop the sigh that releases from my chest as I pull the comforter back around my upper body.

My hips start to roll and grind in concert to his agile tongue, he works it tirelessly over my swollen clit as his hands constantly stroke my sensitive skin. Reaching down, I grasp his head and pull him in tighter, not caring about anything other than my next orgasm.

The sudden thrust of his finger into my pussy, sends me over the edge and I start shuddering when my release hits.

"I made a plan for today and you aren't going to like it," he tells me as I lay there, heavy-lidded and pleased to find he's somehow re-burrito'd me.

"Okay, that's fine," I mumble until I make sense of his words. "Wait! What?"

He barks out a laugh, roughly kissing me when I glare at him.

"That isn't fair. You made me come." Shit, if that's the best argument I can muster up, he's really done a number on me. "Rewind. What's your plan?"

"I'm not leading your family back to your sister and the Knights. Felix will have run my plates by now, they're registered to a dummy address in southern Arizona, so that shouldn't be an issue, but they'll have spotters out for us."

His logic is sound, I think as I let out a huge yawn. "And?"

"I talked to Parker and he agreed, you and I are going to wait out this family meeting of yours up at my grandfather's old cabin," he tells me. "Once that's past, I'll take you to your sister and you decide what to do with the broach you swiped."

"It's not stealing if it... Oh, never mind. I'm not just going to run and hide with you; I can deal with Felix." At least I can if it's just the two of us, that weasel has spent years hiding behind others.

"It isn't just Felix that bothers me, it's the rest of those psychos you're related to. Like it or not, this isn't a discussion. Piper is pregnant, remember? Parker will not have her placed in harm's way." Tin's voice is determined and his eyes show that he's ready to do battle over this.

As I silently weigh the pros and cons to his plan, I remember our earlier discussion and how he spoke about Ransom and Joey as if they were his own. As much as I dislike having him dictate my actions, I don't doubt his intentions.

"What did Piper have to say about this?" I ask him, not quite ready to give in so easily.

"He's probably breaking the news to her now," he answers, twisting the corner of his mouth as if trying to contain a grin. "She tends to get her way when she wants something though, so stay tuned."

"Apparently I'm a captive audience," I sass back.

"I'll make it up to you."

The look on his face leaves no doubt how he intends to do that.

Tin

We get loaded up and head out. With a new destination in mind, we finally getting back on the interstate to cut across Nevada. Shifting my eyes over to Paige, I decide to wait until I have some privacy to make that call.

I wasn't expecting the turn that last night took, but I am definitely looking forward to the next couple of weeks enjoying Paige's company. Not that I don't have some questions about her family.

"Paige," I keep my voice low, hoping she's had enough coffee to be amenable to this conversation. "I was wondering about the, I don't know what to call it, hierarchy? Of your family."

"Okay," she says, keeping her head on the road in

front of us as the mask I've seen several times, slides across her face.

"Does your mom call the shots? Exactly how many siblings does she have and what is their pecking order in making decisions?"

"We're not the fucking mafia, Tin," she sighs, sounding completely exasperated. "And my mom *wishes* she was in charge."

"Like I said, Tober told us some things when he was with us, but he doesn't exactly talk—well, not in a straight line, let's say. I was almost more confused after our talks than before."

"Tober's mom is my mom's oldest sister. She holds the most control, mostly because her husband heads a security team of sorts."

"Oh, of course. Nothing like the mafia at all." I nod my head, more interested in keeping my eyes on the vehicles around us than arguing over what level of criminal enterprise her family is.

"Do you want the breakdown or are you going to practice your stand-up routine?" Paige asks, giving me the I'm-kind-of-annoyed-kind-of-amused look, I've become much too familiar with the past few days.

"I apologize, I will not interrupt again," I promise, pushing my lips together to show her I mean it.

"Tober's mom, Betta, married some Russian

super-human, military guy. They have three other kids besides Tober. Then my mom's brother has like seven or eight kids, but he never married. Next, there's our mom," Paige pauses when she gets to her own family unit. "It took me years of wading through bullshit, but I think our dad was like her third or fourth cousin. They were supposed to create a stronger alliance between one of the *competitive* branches of the family."

"But your mom killed him?" I query when she pauses to drink some water.

"She killed him, she killed her younger sister—Felix's mom, she's probably killed a lot of people. The worst kept secret is that my mom and Felix's dad have been fucking for years. Felix is my youngest aunt's oldest child, and probably ruthless enough to take over."

"You could have taken it, right?" I ask, truly wondering how far down the rabbit hole she was before Piper roped her into living together and Paige started writing. "You could have taken control of your line?"

"If I'm being honest? Yes and no," Paige whispers.

"Strictly between you and me, I'll never bring it up again or tell another soul. Will you explain your answer?"

"I could have taken over our line of the family. Yes. But I never could have held it without Piper." Paige looks out the window to her right, waiting long moments before continuing. "Piper is extremely successful as a consultant because the client can explain issues they're facing and she can almost instantly assess the fastest way to the desired outcome."

"So, she's playing chess while most people are playing checkers?"

"No. You, Felix, me, and my *living* aunts and uncles are playing chess, successfully, mind you. We're all above-average intelligence-wise," she says, twirling her forefinger in a circle and I'm pleased with her unprovoked compliment. Despite the people she lumped me in with. "Meanwhile, Piper is playing Chess, Tetris, and Stratego, while applying nail polish without a single smudge."

"You're giving a lot of credit to someone who cannot tell a lie and is, genuinely, the kindest person I've ever met." The words slip out of me, unguarded and Paige lets out a gasp.

"Are you in love with her?" she asks, tilting her head to study me.

"No. I mean, I think she's hot, but Piper and I have very different personalities."

"Aww, you're blushing," Paige laughs, reaching up to tap my cheek bone. "And thank you."

"For what?"

"You think I'm hot!"

"Not as hot as she is," I say, shrugging my shoulder. Which was something I could easily do before she slugged the hell out of it.

"In some ways, I want to be a little more like Piper," Paige says after leaning over to kiss the area she just walloped. "And in some ways, she needs to be a little more like me."

"I heard her talking to Joey after that book thing, what was it? Motorcycles, Mayhem, Mafia?" I ask, certain I'm saying that wrong, but she waves at me to continue. "Piper said she had to 'channel' you to get through the day. That she had to push herself into something uncomfortable, but once she did, she really had fun. I think you owe her a another signing though, she really wanted to experience it with you."

Paige looks at me for a moment or two before answering. "Now, are you saying that because you care about Piper and me, or because you know that Joey wants to go to a signing and you want me to bring her along also?"

"Yes."

"That was an either-or, not a multiple-choice

question," Paige replies, crossing her arms over her chest.

"Hey, look at the restaurants up here. What do you say we grab a bite and stretch out our legs?"

"Sure, how about a *chicken* sandwich?" Paige snaps back, her voice laced in sarcasm.

Which I deserve.

FIVE

Tin

Sitting across the table from Paige, I'm still trying to rectify her earlier comment about Piper. But I can't even decide on the best line of questioning.

"What's bothering you?" she finally asks me.

"You make Piper sound diabolical. I'll concede she's intelligent, but I don't know that I can see her running laps around the group of people you listed off," I tell her, picking up my milkshake even though I know I'll regret having this much dairy later on.

"You'll just have to take my word on that, I guess," Paige says shrugging her shoulders.

"Really? That's all you're going to give me?"

"Chicks before dicks." She nods, giving me a little grin.

"Now where have I heard that before?" I shake my head, knowing that Piper once used that line on Parker.

"We're heading there now, but there doesn't seem to be any sign of them," I tell Parker, having called to check in with him later that night.

Keeping my eyes on the well-lit store, I watch for Paige to re-emerge from the restroom tucked back in the corner.

"I don't like that at all," he says. "They're not just going to throw in the towel and stop looking for her. I've reached out to enough *friendlies* in the area, that someone should have seen them."

I nod my head even though he can't see, glad he let the Battle Born MC know I'd be driving through their territory. "Paige pulled the sim card from her phone earlier, so I don't see them getting ahead of us, but at this point, I'm just going to drive straight through."

"Stay frosty and let me know if you want me to send someone up to watch your back. Otherwise,

TIN

I'm keeping the guys close to home for the time being."

"Hey, did Piper know anything else about this *family meeting?*" I ask him, having previously filled him in on the basics of what Paige had told me.

"No. She did say there is a box of documents that she found in a crawl space of their house, but that other than skimming through the first few pages, she didn't have the time or energy to do anything other than to shove them back where she found them," he responds. "If her great-aunt left more information behind, my guess would be it's in there, I just don't know that it's worth making the trip for it right now."

"Especially since they periodically watch that house," I agree, remembering the car full of guys that Parker saw the one night he spent there. "Your call, of course."

"Speaking of my call, Piper wants to talk to Paige so grab a burner and call this number tomorrow morning after ten," he tells me before rattling off the number of what has to be the burner he got for Piper.

"After ten? What do you two do, lay around in bed all morning? You're going to get soft." I can't help but to give him shit over that while I jot down the number on a receipt I find in the armrest.

"Fuck off. Piper is working remotely, and since the company is based on the east coast, she starts around six and then, usually, has some free time around ten. Anything else on your mind, smart ass?"

"You know you're really sensitive when you're expecting, don't you?" That only elicits a grunt from him, so I get serious again. "What do you say I ask Red if he'd ride out and collect that box."

"That a favor he owes you or one that you'll owe him?" he asks me, knowing full well that the older my brother gets, the more he tries to find ways to strengthen our bond. "Alright then, if you want to work that out and I'll ask Piper where to find the box."

When he disconnects, I scroll through my contacts until I find who I'm looking for.

"Tin! I heard you were up our way," Tank's voice comes in loud and clear even over all the background noise I can hear around him.

"Just passing through, unfortunately."

"We heard you might have some trouble on your six, anything Kat can help with?" he asks, and I laugh. His Ol' Lady is a hired killer, but I don't think the situation is that dire. Just then I see Paige strolling through the store, obviously picking up some junk food and sodas for the ride.

"Nothing I can't handle, man. We'll catch up on my next ride," I promise him.

"I don't know, Tin. Kat was hoping for some action."

"Tell her I appreciate it, and give her a kiss from me. Wherever you think is appropriate."

"Asshole," he laughs, knowing I mean nothing by it.

As we get back on the road to my grandfather's cabin, Paige and I discuss sending Red out to Oklahoma. Once she agrees, I decide to trust her to send the text off to my brother, because that whole voice-to-text thing is beyond me.

I give her side-eye a moment later when Red's name pops up on my truck's system. Her lips twitch, so I know I'm going to be in for it now.

"What?" I answer the call.

"Are you drunk?" Red responds and I grunt, raising an eyebrow at Paige.

She blows me a kiss.

"Red, meet Paige. Paige, Red. I asked her to send you a text I dictated, not take artistic liberties," I say, more for his benefit than hers.

"What can I say? I'm a writer," she sasses back, throwing her hands in the air.

"Huh. Well, I'm actually on my way back from

Florida now. I can be there in two or three days," he tells me.

"Shit, are you riding or driving?"

"Driving. It'll be late when I pull in, does anyone mind if I crash at the house for the night?" he asks us.

"Not at all," Paige answers his question before giving him the code for the garage door and lets him know that the door leading into the house will be unlocked. "Are you going to come up to your grandfather's cabin once you get it? It would be, ah, interesting, to meet you."

Her question is met by silence and I let out a heavy sigh.

"She means old man Clifford's place," I tell him, belatedly realizing that while I considered the man family, Red never really knew the old man who lived next door to us when we were younger, and I hadn't gotten around to explaining that to Paige. "It's in Utah, I'll text you the location once you find the box. Oh, and keep your eyes peeled around the house and when you leave it. Paige's family is hunting for her and her sister."

"Oh, goody. I haven't had any fun since Me'ansome's brother kidnapped Joey. The second time, that is. Talk soon," he tells us before disconnecting the call.

"Me'ansome's brother kidnapped his own niece? Twice?" Paige asks and I grunt. "Do tell."

"It's not relevant," I let her know. The guy's been cremated and flushed down a toilet, so it's safe to say he's no longer a danger to anyone.

"Do you and Red have different grandparents?" she asks me next.

"Naw. Mr. Clifford was our neighbor when we were kids, he was disabled in the Vietnam War and hated most of the people in our neighborhood, but my parents most of all," I tell her, keeping my eyes on constant lookout for cops and any other tails.

"Oh, your charming personality won him over, didn't it?" Her voice is dripping with sarcasm as she bats her eyes at me.

"Something like that," I say, preferring to keep things light between us.

"And what, no one noticed when he left Maine with you? Oh! Did he kidnap you?" her eyes light up at that thought and I'm beginning to get nervous about how excited she becomes when a story takes a dark turn.

"No one cared. The whole neighborhood was scooped up by a developer when I was about sixteen or so. Mr. Clifford bought an RV, planning on spending the rest of his life seeing America. My parents moved and left me a box of my things, so when he invited me along it seemed like as good as plan as any."

I stop talking, trying to remember if I had ever shared this much with anyone other than Parker or Ransom, and I doubt I have.

Paige

One thing I know from first-hand experience is what it's like when you share a truth with another person—a truly deep part of yourself—and they don't respond how you expect.

It's very rare that I freeze up around others. I was taught early on how to read people's emotions and what reaction is best in each situation. Not for any altruistic reason, nope, I was expected to find their weakness and exploit them.

I don't want to do that to Tin, though.

Which leaves me in a position I've never been in with anyone. How do I respond as someone who cares about him?

I wish Piper was here. My shortcomings in this area need actual advice and not the secret code we developed when we were ten years old. When she talks to people, she always manages to ask really insightful questions; I close my eyes and try to imagine what she would have gleaned from what Tin just shared.

"When did you first call Clifford your grandfather? Not out loud, but in your mind?"

He cocks his head to the side, as he considers the question and I feel like I've done Piper justice.

"About a year or so before we took off in the RV. He had hired me on, having me run errands for him or help with chores around his house. And that winter my parents had missed some bills and our gas had been turned off. It turned into a shitshow and for whatever reason the cops came out.

"One of them was ready to call Child Protective Services, and I knew enough to know that me, at that age and the size I was—well, it would have been a death sentence," he says, occasionally pausing to drink some of his coffee. "Clifford had been away at some reunion for his squad, I think, and pulled up in the middle of it. He took one of the officers aside and the next thing I know, I spent the next month sleeping on his couch."

"Only the next month?" I wonder at the timing of it as I studying Tin's body, trying to imagine him as he was then.

Height-wise, he's average, but his lithe body is muscular from head to toe. Not the overly large muscles you see from long hours spent lifting, but a hard body from years of physical work. Mentally, I strip away his muscles and an inch or so, to understand why a group home would have broken him.

"Yeah, once dad got caught up with his bills he insisted I move back because he was worried about the welfare checks that Mom was getting for me."

"Hmm, but the RV life wasn't all it was cracked up to be?"

"I liked it well enough, traveling at least. Clifford got tired of it during the first year, so he sold it and bought a cabin. After that, he made me finish off high school and I got hired on with a roofing crew after that, enough with the twenty questions now," he grumbles, and I know it's more that he's not used to talking about himself than to try to push me away.

"I'd like to take some college level classes," I say, feeling like I should share something of myself. "I think my writing would benefit from it, and I'm horrible at graphic design, so I think some of those classes could also be helpful."

"Why don't you give me some of your books and I'll let you know what I think?" His grin is way too sly for me to think he's being serious for a moment.

"If you're looking for pointers, I'm happy to critique you the next time we fuck," I tell him.

"You didn't seem to have any complaints, so let's just leave it at that," Tin says.

"Maybe I was faking it?"

"You weren't, not if you're talking about fucking me again."

Damn, he has a point there.

Settling into the cabin he inherited is easier than I expected. When we aren't enjoying each other's bodies, he's working on projects around the property and I work on my books. Plural, because while I may have upcoming deadlines, sometimes I get wild ideas and am ten thousand words into a new story before I focus on what I need to.

While I am trying to keep a low profile online, I jump on social media and notice I've missed a few messages from another author that I'm friends with, so I reach out to her.

Kristine Allen writes MC romance, like I do, but she also has a series that revolves around hockey players that I love.

She was a little miffed about not getting to spend more time with me at the MMM signing and the only way I knew to fix that was to let her in on my little secret. She got such a hoot out of finding out that I twisted my twin sister's arm into covering for me, that I can't help but to share the news of my impending 'auntie' status.

I'm waiting for her next message when Tin clears his throat.

"Want to go into town with me?" he asks when I look up. "Figured we could use more groceries for when Red gets here and I need to hit the hardware store."

"Sure!" I readily accept, getting slightly stir-crazy at this point. "Ugh, when did it start raining?"

"A couple of hours ago," he grins, already knowing how focused I get when I open my laptop.

The closest town to the cabin probably has less than ten thousand people in the off-season, being one of hundreds of ski towns throughout the west. The drive takes us longer than the time spent at the stores we need and I'm happy that the rain has tapered off so I can see more of the area on our way back to the cabin.

"This place is magical," I tell him. "No plans to sell the cabin, I hope?"

"No, I do rent it out during the peak season," he replies with a proud grin. "That pays for its upkeep and taxes, so there's no reason to let it go.

"Maybe you can show me around some more tomorrow," I suggest as he pulls into the driveway.

"We'll see when Red gets here." His answer dodges any commitment and I slide out of my seat without looking at him, figuring he can get the few bags that we have.

Eww. I look down and grimace at the mud coating half of my shoes.

"Hey, watch out for the puddles," I say seconds before I hear a loud splat.

"Son of a bitch!" Tin yells and I turn to see him still holding the plastic bags in the air above his shoulders, but he's down with one knee mired in the mud.

I can't stop the snort that escapes me, nor a laugh after his eyes shoot daggers at me.

"I warned you," I insist, raising my hands in the air in an effort to make peace.

Of course, that goes right out of the window when he starts to stand up and his leg once again slips. This time the handles of the bags slide from his grasp as he tries, too late, to catch himself.

With another *splat*, he ends up flat on his chest and this time there's no controlling my laughter.

"Come help me up?" The calm timber of his voice does not match the look in his eyes, so I take a step backward, then another when I see his body tense as his muscles coil and I turn to run.

Darn it! I seriously misjudged how far I was from

the porch and try to make it to the stairs in a few clumsy leaps, but can feel him nearly behind me and know I have no chance of getting inside without him on my heals.

Darting to the right, I full out sprint to try to make it to the back door with enough distance between us that I can lock him out—at least until he cools down. I know that looking backward will only slow me down, but I decide to chance a glance once I've round the second corner of the house.

I'm instantly confused when I don't see him.

"Oof!" The wind is knocked out of me as I'm turning my head forward and make contact with Tin's muddy body. "Crap!"

"What? You were laughing a minute ago, isn't it still funny?" he mocks me as his mud-covered hand reaches up to cup my face.

"You're an asshole," I sputter, trying to break free from his arm that's tightly securing me to his body.

"I thought we'd established that shortly after we met?" Bending down, he has me in a fireman's carry before I know what he's thinking and turns to retrace the mud splatters left by his boots, up the back steps and through the kitchen. "Shower time."

Holding onto his belt for purchase, I see no point in arguing about that. I'll save my breath in case he tries to get out of cleaning up the trail he left from the front door straight on through to where he caught me near the back door.

I no sooner get my clothes off and slide under the spray that Tin had turned on, than I remember the groceries that were left behind. Opening my mouth, I look at him to say something as he follows me into the shower, but the sight of his body stops me.

It seems like his cock is swelling with each step he takes, closing the distance between us.

"They'll keep," he says, reading my mind as he leans down, pressing his lips against mine.

"Uh, huh," I moan against his lips, eyeing the body wash on the shelf behind him. When I reach for it, he holds his hand out and I pour some for him before I fill up the center of my palm. Without a word, we both start cleaning each other's bodies; using the time to explore and learn about each other.

Coming to a jagged scar on his back, I trace it before tapping it, silently asking him for an explanation.

"Bar fight. Mexico," he says before pausing. "Wait, no, Mexico was the one on my thigh. That was New Jersey."

Cocking an eyebrow, I lean back, trying to locate the scar on his thigh. Wouldn't you know it was just below his ball sack?

"Did you get too close to someone's wife?" I ask with a grin.

"Nah, I got too close to someone's mistress."

I click my tongue and shake my head.

"Yeah, and she got pissed when she found me fucking her sister, so she told her brother, and he came at me later that night. Me'ansome managed to save the business side of it, but I stay away from that whole crazy bunch nowadays."

"Oh, they're the crazy ones?" I ask, as I wash his balls.

"Considering what you're holding, I am happy to concede that I have my moments."

"Wise man," I sass back before lowering myself to my knees.

While his body blocks most of the water coming from the showerhead, it still runs down and over us as I wrap my lips around his half hard dick, swirling my tongue around the head as I bob up and down on it.

Keeping my eyes tightly closed against the water running over us, I focus my attention on his frenulum and notice the hitch in his breathing the light caress of my tongue causes. On a hunch, I slide my left hand further back from where I've been caressing his balls and rub the pad of my finger along his taint.

"Christ, woman," he growls, leaning forward to brace himself against the wall.

"Hey!" a man's voice shouts from down the hall. "Tin, fucking answer me. I've got my gun out."

Tin's hand reaches down, moving my head back into place when I started to scramble away.

"We're fine, Red, go away!" Tin bellows back before lowering his voice. "Don't stop, Paige. I'm so close."

SIX

Tin

"Glad to see you're still alive," Red says when I make it downstairs. "Fucking groceries were on the ground outside, doors were wide open, and mud all through the place."

"We got a little sidetracked." I shrug, narrowing my eyes at him when Paige saunters down the stairs, still drying her hair off with a towel.

"What the hell have you done?" he says and while any number of responses float through my mind, I decide to put him at ease; it's the least I can do after the errand he just ran for me.

"I guess you've met Piper? This is her sister, Paige," I tell him and smother a grin at the expressions the flint across his face.

"Shit. I thought you had started a war," he deeply exhales and sits down heavily on the nearest chair. "What is it with the Kings and twins?"

"It's weird, right?" I crack a grin in agreement.

"Well, I got that box you asked for and your groceries are on the counter." Red's eyes are on Paige as he touches the corner of the rectangular box. "These guys that are following you, they partial to Cadillac's?"

"That sounds about right," Paige replies, her fingers dance over the top of the box as if suddenly anxious to see the contents.

"They were on me shortly after I left your house and I lost them two different times, they were persistent alright."

"Thank you," she says, pulling open the flaps and frowning at the mess of papers within. "They don't have much time left, between now and the meeting, so I'm sure they're getting testy."

"Why don't you start checking out what's in there?" I ask her, hoping like hell she doesn't want me prying through it. "I could use Red's help out back."

While he looks less than enthusiastic, at her nod, Red takes my hint and follows me outside.

"Just so we're clear, I'm not cleaning these floors," Paige calls out to our backs.

"She your Ol' Lady?" Red asks me next.

"Nope."

"She sure sounds like an Ol' Lady." He snorts at his own joke. "Easy on the eyes, though."

Less than an hour later when I hear my truck start up, Red and I look at each other dumbfounded before I run inside and find her short note:

Sorry for swiping your phone and truck, I need a few days to handle this.
I'll find my way back to Piper.

"She must have realized she's way too good looking for you," Red says from over my shoulder, and I turn to glare at him. "Are we going after her or I am taking you back home?"

"Home," I say after a moment, and I can see the shocked look on his face before he mumbles something and turns away from me.

It takes me longer to mop away the mud than it does to pack up the few things I had with me. Grabbing the box and Paige's large backpack last, I lock up the cabin and climb into Red's SUV.

While my curiosity is getting the better of me, I am a hundred percent certain that Paige left the family jewel with me. My eyes fell on her backpack almost instantly after reading that damned note and knowing that it could make all the difference in keeping her safe; I knew I shouldn't track her ass down.

No matter how much I wanted to.

Paige

It takes a special kind of man that will tap down on every instinct he has and simply do what he's asked.

Looking in the rear-view mirror, I hold my breath, waiting to see if Tin can be *that* man.

That broach needs to be as far away from me as possible, when I go to talk to my cousin.

In a way, Piper was right, the key to our future was held in our past.

If I had come across a box of old papers, I would have dumped it. No hesitation.

Instead, I sat down at Tin's small dining table and began pulling out a handful of papers at a time. I immediately started sorting it into different stacks: minutia, photos, love letters between Aunt Tiff and the man who, I assume, became her husband.

I barely glanced at the letters, but I carefully laid them out, thinking they might come in handy for a historical romance. That was when my eyes happen upon a line that sparked my interest.

...you must understand. This has to be handled a certain way and as the owner of the necklace that Father gifted me, I have to deal with it at the family meeting this fall. I can't marry you or risk becoming pregnant in the meanwhile—because once I have an heir, the decision becomes theirs.

Hmm. I quickly flip through the box and pull out anything that looks like more of their letters, but nothing seems to be relevant.

Skimming the letters, my heart goes out to this great-aunt of mine. She and her secret fiancé had so many hopes and dreams, that they eagerly shared with each other in each letter.

This is what life is supposed to be like, I think to myself, as I dig into the box and come up with a bound book that's wrapped in some type of rough cloth.

I carefully unwrap it while I continue to think about the woman who spoke about wanting children, moving to her fiancé's hometown, and living a life she could be proud of. To my knowledge, she never had a child; I can't imagine she would have left the house to us—oh, Piper, actually—if she did.

As I open the cover of the book, several dried flowers slide out and I carefully put them in the cloth that I had laid to the side.

I flip to the next page and my eyes widen at the neatly handwritten words, *About my family*. My heart skips another beat at the next page, knowing that I've hit the jackpot we were hoping for.

Tiff meticulously details the pact that her father made each of his four daughters swear to. The more I read, the more I start to realize what a twisted fuck our great-great-grandfather was.

Suddenly, the truth hits me right in the heart and I want nothing more than to scream in pain, like some wounded animal. The alleged family creed that we were raised to believe in, to serve—is all based on the psychotic mind of this long dead man.

He never wanted the best for any of his daughters, nor their issue. My great-great-grandfather did nothing but sow mistrust and jealousy among his children, literally not caring about any of them.

According to the words in front of me, it was his idea that if a member of the family betrayed the others, then the person closest to them had to be the one to kill them.

I've known my entire life that Piper was the smartest person I knew, but I always chalked her inability to succeed at the cons we were taught to her honest nature, now I suspect she failed spectacularly so no one would care when she walked away.

Thinking back to all the conversations we had from childhood on, when she tried to convince me that what we were being taught was wrong. It was years later, when I accepted her offer to live in Aunt Tiff's house, that I understand the basis of what she tried to impart was that the marks weren't the enemy, our family was.

Briefly, my eyes flick over to see what's left in the box and in the corner, there's a blue velvet box that I reach for; momentarily surprised at the weight of it. Opening it, I frown, wondering how the tiny pair of baby shoes could account for what I just felt. Lifting those out and frowning when I see they had been worn at some point, I notice a tab that they had been hiding and I tug on that.

I let out a gasp, recognizing the first item that tumbles out. It's my family's broach, and under it, I see the ring, necklace, and earrings that account for each of the other family branches' gems.

Holding up the piece that I'm most familiar with, I'm instantly convinced it's just a copy, two of the other three pieces seem to be also. The fourth piece, though, that's the one that doesn't appear to have any flaws. It must have been the piece she allegedly surrendered, giving up her place in the family.

Looking back at her book, I flip through it until I find confirmation that she had, indeed, had copies made of the four pieces that represent the crest of each of the original four sisters.

And then, on the page explaining the duplicates

she had commissioned, I find the information she had alluded to in her letter to the man she later married.

I immediately look around for a phone and spot Tin's laying on the counter behind me. Some other time, I'll have a talk with him about not unlocking his phone in plain sight of anyone around him, but today that works in my favor.

Dialing the burner that I spoke to Piper on the other day, she immediately answers.

"Did Red get there?"

"I don't have time to talk right now. Please, just tell me where Tober is," I ask her, trying to keep my voice calm.

She immediately rattles off the name of some ranch before telling me the town and state.

"Okay. I'll call you in a few days," I tell her.

"Paige!" she calls out, stopping me from hanging up. "Don't get dead."

"Have a little faith."

SEVEN

Tin

Within an hour of leaving my cabin, I contacted Parker on a fresh burner, letting him know the situation.

By nightfall, I was back home and seething. Sneaking looks at Paige's backpack like it would detonate any moment.

At midnight, I had enough. I tore into the bag and down near the bottom I located a wooden box with intricate carvings all around it.

I kept it next to my bed; finally getting some sleep, but my patience was at an end when I still hadn't gotten an update the next morning.

Reaching over, I shifted the gold latch and opened the box.

Well, fuck me.

Not worth anything?

Sentimental value only?

She better not be expecting a ring from me. The errant thought takes me by surprise, but dammit, I've come to enjoy her company. And if I'm going to be with someone, I'd rather it be with someone who isn't boring and can accept me as I am.

I pick up the broach and hold it up for closer inspection, trying to remember everything I learned when representing a jeweler a few years back. Even if I'm only partially correct, this thing has got to be worth a half million, easy.

Taking a deep breath, I replace the broach in the box and bring it over to my safe. On second thought, I put it under the sink in the bathroom.

No one will look for it there.

"Hey, can I swing by and talk to Piper?" I ask Me'ansome when he picks up on the first ring.

"You gonna upset her?" he counters.

"That's not my intention. I just need a clearer picture of what's happening."

"Pick up breakfast on the way," he says before hanging up.

Sitting around the island in his kitchen is, almost, like it has been thousands of times before. With the exception of his Ol' Lady.

Although I've known her for months now, I keep sneaking looks at her; trying to pick out differences between her and Paige.

The one similarity that I do notice is how aware they both are of their surroundings. I doubt the average person would spot it, but both Paige and Piper are subtly aware of everyone's movements around them and of noises outside the house.

Just now it was Piper's eyes quickly bouncing between Me'ansome to the front of the house, that was the first notice I had of Ransom's bike approaching the house—and she damn well heard it first, but discounted any danger after correctly identifying the sound that it makes.

Crossing behind her, I momentarily pause, pretending to look at something out the back window and within a handful of seconds, Piper has shifted so I'm no longer standing in her blind spot.

That goddamn family did a number on these girls, alright. But at the end of the day, living in the world that Me'ansome and I do, awareness is a good trait to have.

"Me'ansome, I know Tin has some questions for me, but I don't know that Ransom needs to..." Piper stops talking, giving him a shrug instead of completing her thought.

"Why don't you two move the conversation to your office? I'm sure Ransom will be more interested in finishing off this food," Me'ansome suggests.

With a smile, Piper snags another piece of bacon before kissing her Old Man and tilting her head at me, silently telling me to follow her.

We're just about to the room she now has a desk and computer set up in, when the front door opens and Ransom immediately comments on the lingering smell of breakfast.

I leave the door open behind me, as I turn the chair from the other desk in the room. The decidedly low-tech items on its worn surface, let me know that Parker pushed his desk into the corner to make room for Piper's things.

"Can I see the note she left you?" Piper asks me and I reach into my pocket to pull it out. I don't miss the smile that flits across her face and I frown, wondering what caused that.

She barely looks at the words once she unfolds the paper and places it on the corner of her desk.

"Paige is interesting, isn't she?" Piper's rhetorical question gets a smile from me.

"And infuriating," I answer, shrugging my shoulders. "Occasionally funny, really good cook though."

"Did you go through the box?"

"No, I figure she took what she needed from it when she left. I know that your great-aunt walked away from the family business, so to speak, but I need to know two things," I tell her and she tilts her head to the side waiting for me to continue. "If she finds a way to remove your mom, aunts, and uncles from the pact, or whatever it is, will they come after the two of you?"

"No, the remaining two lines become responsible for our protection," she replies, and her answer removes a weight from my shoulders. "It's in their best interest, since they each hope to be the last line left *in the game*."

"What is there like a grand prize or something?" I ask her.

"Is that your second question?"

I let out a whistle and shake my head, surprised that she is going to make me stick to the number I mentioned.

"Had you already gone through the box?"

"No, Tin. I had only come across it shortly before I met Me'ansome, and I was trying to wrap up a project for work. I'm sure you can understand why it slipped my mind," she answers me, gliding a hand down across her slightly round belly, and I have no doubt it's the truth—just maybe not all of it. "Will you answer a question for me?"

"Tell me what you aren't saying and I will."

"There was something curious I came across during the renovations, that might have a bearing on what she's up to. There was a child's drawing that had fallen behind the kitchen cabinet, the house in it was close enough to the one that Aunt Tiff left us. The father had a star covering his chest, like a marshal's badge. The mother had long dark hair and then there was a little boy," she tells me and I raise an eyebrow, not understanding the significance. "I had always heard she never had any children, and if she did have a child, or a grandchild, why was the house and a small sum of money left to me? A distant relative she had only met once."

"Do you love her?" Piper decides to pack a wallop with her question.

"The answer is as complicated as your sister," I tell her, carefully avoiding Piper's eyes when I reach out to snag the note on my way out of her office.

Feeling suddenly cross, I decide to head to my own office and see what work I've been neglecting. It's rare that I have any cases that need to be tried in court, but one can hope.

Paige

I made it up to the ranch that Tober found work on and was actually impressed with the scope of the operation. Sitting across the road from the main entrance, I scroll through the website they have. This place offers everything from counselling with horses to month-long camp sessions to boarding and training.

It's the perfect place for him.

A sudden horn makes me jump and I frown at having let a truck sneak up on me.

"Something I can help you with?" an older man with a gray Stetson calls from the half-open window of a pick-up truck that has seen a lot of wear.

"Oh, I'm sorry, I was trying to find my cousin's number. I wasn't sure if I should just drive up to the barn or what," I tell him, holding up my phone as if it'll provide an alibi for me.

"Well, now, who's your cousin?" he asks, and I notice his smile isn't as wide as it was a moment ago.

"Tober…"

"Why don't you follow me up the drive, I know just where he's working today," the man answers with a puzzled expression on his face.

Passing a modern looking red barn, I follow the

truck to a pasture a little ways beyond it, all the while trying to figure out what the old cowboy's reaction to me means. When he slows to a stop, my eyes follow his extended arm until I look the direction of his pointed finger.

There is absolutely no mistaking Tober for anyone else. The man is built like an ox. I throw my somewhat stolen truck into park and slide out of it. Waving my thanks to the cowboy, I walk toward the fence line.

A loud *Woop!* makes me stop in my tracks for a moment, until I realize it was just Tober spotting me. He's running straight across the field at me, with a huge grin and I put my hand up to my brow, blocking the sun as it hits my face.

Just as suddenly as he started toward me, Tober stops about thirty feet away and studies me.

"I thought you were Piper," he calls out and I have absolutely no idea how he was able to tell us apart from so far away.

"We need to talk, Tober. I think I know a way we can all be free of them."

"I'm gonna have to ask you to leave, Paige," the cowboy says, casually standing next to his truck with one thumb resting in his belt. Except there's nothing casual about the way his shoulders are squared off, or that he somehow knows who I am.

I stand there, studying him and looking back over to Tober as the pieces click together in my mind. I can't help but to smile when my eyes flick down to his boots; the last pair of his shoes that I saw were significantly smaller.

"If you're who I'm guessing you are, Piper and I have as much right to our freedom as your mother did. And we can't attain that without Tober, can we?"

"From what I've always heard about you, you're more likely to take control than to give it up." He responds, not denying his parentage.

"Considering I was taught cons your mother created, instead of nursery rhymes, I'd think if anyone was going to cut me a break, it should be her son." I once again try to get confirmation about his identity, but he just stares me down for long moments.

Dammit, I just want to scream and pull Tober away—to force him to do what I need him to do. Thankfully, he's managed to find, what seems to be the only part of our family that actually knows how to create a caring environment.

My heart breaks a little, wondering what it would have been like if mom had hidden us away and cared enough to let us grow up away from all of her siblings.

"Is Piper's baby alright?" Tober asks once he makes it to the other side of the fence.

"Yes." I turn to look at him and chance a step closer. "She's having twins and even before I knew that she was pregnant, I knew that your mom was getting frustrated with us. If I had completed my last job, as planned, I think she would have had me killed.

"Piper is special, Tober, I think you believe that too. I thought that life away from the family would be boring, but it isn't; Piper has shown me that. I just don't know how else to get them to leave us alone." I plead with him, hoping that he'll give me the chance to explain my plan.

"Pops?" I spin around, frustrated that I let my emotions cloud my senses, allowing another man to come up behind me. "She isn't wrong, so why don't we hear her out?"

Looking at the older man, I point at the guy behind me to emphasize his point, and try to keep a neutral but hopeful look on my face.

"He's still wet behind the ears and hasn't met your ilk before," the cowboy says, staring daggers at his son.

"Tober's told me all about them, but she seems to be putting her sister first, so let's just hear her out." His voice remains firm as he squares his own shoulders in almost a mirror image of his father. "I'm Nick, by the way. My dad is Earl."

"Break room," Earl breaks in as I'm about to smile in relief at having found an ally. "I assume you were careful about not being followed?"

"Yes, sir. And I borrowed the truck," I answer him, getting a huff from him at the word *borrowed*, compelling me to clarify. "From a friend."

After I grab Tiff's journal from my truck, I follow Earl back to the red barn and look around, fairly certain that the ring covered the cost of this whole operation, no matter that my family said she had to surrender it, but that it was Earl who made this ranch profitable.

"How was she able to keep you a secret?" I ask, as soon as we enter a room that's almost set up classroom style.

Earl's eyes fall on the journal that I'm holding and it's plain to see he recognizes it.

"Is that number five or eight?" he counters, ignoring my question.

When I frown, he reaches for it, but I take a step away from him.

"She numbered them, along the crease in the first page. I have numbers one to four, six, and seven. I don't even know if there is an eight, but I'm missing number five," he tells me, as he takes a seat and gestures to me to do the same.

I wait until Tober and Nick sit down and I take a seat closer to the door before flipping open the book.

"It's number five," I tell Earl and a smile crosses his face for the first time since he greeted me on the road. "You can have it once I finish this thing."

"Well, let's hear your plan," Earl drawls out and I spend the next twenty minutes explaining it to them and answering their questions.

"Damn," Nick says when I've finished. "You've got some balls, don't you?"

"I don't think I can do that," Tober says, staring down at where he's threading his fingers together. "I don't think my mother would let me."

"Why are you here, Tober?" I gently question him, leaning forward in my seat as I hold his gaze with mine.

"Because I don't want to be there anymore." He squirms nervously in his own chair as I furiously try to figure out how to encourage him to do this. "I don't want to do the things they tell me. Like kidnapping Piper. Piper was always nice to me. And I don't want to drive in Las Vegas ever again."

"Piper is a better person than I will ever be, Tober. You know that and these two men I've never met seem to know that." I try to keep the desperation out of my voice, and I start bouncing my knee when I hear it seep in; attracting Earl's undivided attention. I know he's looking for any sign of insincerity, but I've never been so forthright in my life.

"You're somewhat of a legend," Nick cuts in with a lopsided grin on his face.

"Piper and I want the chance that your grandmother had," I answer, momentarily cutting my eyes to his face. "Piper deserves to live her own life without them calling in a marker one day. Dammit, I want a chance to change how I've always lived. I have my books now and I want to see where that will lead. And I meet someone that I, uh, can respect."

"Uncle Earl?" Tober's voice is filled with panic and sounds as if he's asking the older man to make the choice for him.

"Tober, this is a big decision for you. And what do I always say about big decisions?" Earl's voice holds no trace of condescension as he guides the gentle giant along.

"Big decisions are best made after a big meal and a good night's sleep," Tober recites that like he's heard it a couple dozen times already.

"Then that's what you should do. And no matter what you decide, I'll have your back," he promises my cousin before turning to me. "Now, why don't we get you set up in one of our cabins for the night and you can come to the big house for dinner with us. Unless you're a vegetarian, then you're on your own."

I can't stop the laugh that bubbles out of me as I remember teasing Tin about that not so long ago. "I'm not, Earl. I'd love to join you—Piper is going to be so jealous that you should probably expect her to come along at some point in the future."

EIGHT

Paige

The next morning, shortly after breakfast, I'm driving back down to the main road with one eye on my rear-view mirror.

As promised, Earl is driving his truck with Tober riding shotgun as we head down to Tahoe to meet up with all the branches of the family. I've insisted, and Earl was quick to agree, that he would not reveal himself.

I can't remember ever going through as many burners as I have in the past couple of weeks, but I use another one to change the location of the meeting—to make it easier on us.

Because, fuck them.

I've been jumping through circles for them my

whole life and by some crazy-ass loophole that I found in Tiff's journal, Tober can override his mother and forfeit our line's place in this insanity.

"Can you really hear me, Uncle Earl," Tober asks for the third time. He's both fascinated and terrified by the two-way transmitter that I found at the pawn shop near the hotel I treated us all to last night.

I can't hear the answer that feeds into his earbud, but it gets a sound laugh out of Tober.

"He calls me Big Toe sometimes," Tober explains to me. "It's because I'm so big. But I won't pretend I have this now. Not until we leave, I can still keep it, right?"

"Absolutely," I promise him. Thinking about the nickname, Big Toe, I don't doubt for a moment that Earl also uses it because he knows that Tober is the rightful *heir* of our family.

My next action surprises me as much as it does him. I reach down and take his hand in mine, walking confidently into the restaurant where I reserved a private room for this shit show.

Tober's father is the first person we see when I open the door to the restaurant. No matter that his eyes shoot daggers our way, just as he opens his mouth to speak, two men I've never seen before intercede on our behalf.

"Please, we're ready to start and everyone is waiting to hear what you have to say," the older of the two states, motioning us on our way while the other man blocks Tober's dad.

When the door opens, I see Tober's mother sitting on one side of a table with Felix on her right. That tells me she has chosen her successor, not that it's her choice to make—according to the journal I found. They've preached to me about the *old ways* my whole life, now I can use those traditions to free us.

We're not two steps into the room when Tober roars, "We denounce our rights!"

Naturally, this draws four additional sets of eyes to us. From the other branches of the family there is a person from both my mother's generation and one from mine. No one seems interested in name tags or introductions so I assume it is that family's leader and the one who will succeed them.

"Concede," I hiss out, low enough for him to hear without embarrassing him in front of the others.

"We concede our rights!" he restates the line as I read it in Tiff's journal.

The smirks are clear on the members of the other two family lines, but it's the look in Tober's mother's eyes that chills me to the bone. Betta must have understood what was going to happen once I did not return the broach to her.

"Everyone here knows my heir cannot make decisions for himself, look at how Paige leads him like a lost lamb," she stands up, waving her hand as if my act of supporting Tober is a weakness to be exploited.

I release his hand and take a step away from him. For a moment, his eyes communicate the betrayal he feels.

Instead of speaking or running from the room like I expect him to, he closes his eyes and I know that Earl is speaking to him, helping him through one of the most difficult moments of his life.

"The broach will be held in surety for the safety of my cousins, Piper and Paige. And me. I want to be safe. We concede all of our family's stated earnings of the past year, in exchange for this and will not seek revenge if our parents are brutally murdered to achieve our safety."

I snort and my jaw drops at his last line. Seems like the big guy decided to spice things up with some creative liberties. No matter if that was something that Earl fed him through his earpiece, I decide then and there to give Tober full credit when I retell the story.

Out of the corner of my eye, I see our other

cousin Felix slink from the room and I try to keep the dread at bay. He'll be trouble on another day.

The three families spend the next hour figuring out the reckoning, but it occurs to me part of the way through, that Betta looks calm and possibly relieved. I pray that it's not my newfound hopefulness that's reading too much into her body language.

Once the ordeal is finished, I carefully bypass my mom and Betta's husband who are pacing a path in the already thin restaurant carpet outside the meeting room. I try to hurry Tober back to the hotel where Earl is waiting for him and say my goodbyes. There's one more gauntlet for me to run through today.

And if I'm being honest, I'm more anxious about my next plan than I was about this meeting.

Tin

My phone dings and I pick it up to see a message from Piper, letting me know that her sister is heading our way and relief floods my bloodstream like adrenaline. Her crazy ass must have succeeded if she's thinks it's safe to drive to Piper.

At least for a moment.

Now I have to figure out how to get her to stay with me.

It was nearly midnight when I hear a vehicle pull up to my house. The engine doesn't shut down and I wonder how long it's going to idle in my driveway. With my forefinger and thumb, I shift the blinds open a crack to see what's happening.

The lights outside the garage cast yellowish light over my truck and I can just make out Paige in the driver's seat. Thankfully alone in the vehicle.

After a brief internal debate, I decide to meet her outside, before she chickens out and drives off.

As soon as I open the door to my house, she slides from the driver's seat, holding my phone and truck keys out to me.

"I'm..."

Sliding my rough hand around her throat seconds before my mouth lands on hers, I cut Paige's words off. Keeping our kiss light at first, my lips almost caressing hers until she moans into my mouth.

Deepening our kiss, I lean into her and shift my thumb from her neck under her chin to shift her head up to the perfect angle. My need to feel like I can control her, even for these few precious moments, nearly consumes me and I nip at her tongue when she slides it into my mouth.

I have plans for that tongue and it has nothing to do with my mouth.

It's moments like this, I'm especially happy there's only one neighbor with a line of sight to my house and thankfully, the truck is parked blocking us from their view.

Putting my hands on her shoulders, I use just enough pressure to let her know what I want. Her eyes open wildly as she looks around and I press my thumb to her mouth when she would speak.

I smile down at her when she concedes to my silent demand; moving my hand to the drawstring of my pajama bottoms, I lower them and reach for my dick, tracing it around her lips until she opens her mouth and sucks me in.

Her hand moves up to replace mine around the base before she releases my meat from her mouth with a pop. Lightly squeezing it as she strokes me, her lips kiss the underside of my dick until she makes it to my balls, taking turns with each, she gently sucks them into her mouth.

Moving back up and forming an O with her mouth, she slides me back inside. Going down the length until her lips meet her hand, she places her small soft fingers against my abdomen as she attempts to take me deeper. When Paige starts to gag, I lace my fingers through her hair and push her back down my length. This isn't meant as punishment, after all.

Her pink tongue licks the head of my cock, her dark eyes look up at me and I see the need in them. I imagine it's like looking into a mirror at this point, I think, as I feel my balls harden with cum when she flattens her tongue along the underside and bobs up and down on me again.

Knowing I don't have much time before I explode, I pull her up and push her face first, against the truck. Thankfully, she's wearing a skirt, so I can easily kick her feet further apart and draw her thong to the side.

I go balls deep with one hard thrust and reach around to pinch her clit, as she clamps her pussy tightly around me.

"Fuck, woman," I mutter. "I want all of this greedy cunt of yours, understand?"

She practically mewls as she pushes her ass against me.

"Rub yourself," I demand, grabbing her hand to replace mine over her clit.

Keeping one hand on her hip, I twist my other hand through her long hair and jerk it back, giving my lips easy access to her neck and I really start to drive my big cock into her wet heat.

Paige's moans almost echo through the night as I savagely thrust in and out of her, until she starts to tremble and shake—giving me permission to explode inside her pussy.

I'm gasping for breath when I collapse against her, pinning her to my truck.

"Stay here with me," I say, when I can talk.

"For how long?" she tentatively asks me, and I understand what she really wants to know.

Pulling out of her body, there's no hope for the mess as I pull up my pajamas and turn to the house.

"Permanently."

Walking up the short path, I know this has to be her decision. I leave the door open and go back to bed, smiling a few moments later when I hear the door close and the bolt slide shut.

"We have to talk about you leaving doors open," she says from the doorway to my room, dropping her bag on the floor before taking off her shirt and sliding her skirt down. "From now on, we close and lock them, the windows, too. I don't care if you live in the middle of nowhere, that's just not something I can adjust to."

"Deal. As long as you'll wait until I figure out where the keys are before you start locking things up," I respond, pulling the covers back on the other side of my bed.

"I prefer to think you're giving me shit. Don't mess with that illusion," she sighs, sliding in and across to the middle. I tuck the blanket around her backside as she snuggles against me.

"I'll get you the other comforter tomorrow, I'm too fucking tired now." I promise her, knowing how she likes to be burrito'd when she sleeps.

She places a soft kiss on the skin closest to where her head is laying and seems to fall asleep immediately.

NINE

Paige

I gradually notice the sound of Tin's motorcycle coming up the road and hurry to complete my thoughts on the paragraph I've been staring at for the past ten minutes.

He must be more inspiring than I realized because I pound out a few sentences that will take the book in a direction I wasn't expecting. The front door opens just as I hit 'save' and turn my head to smile at him. "Hey, babe!"

"I got this for you," Tin says, handing me a cut before moving to put the groceries bags on the counter and slowly putting each item away.

Unfolding it, I suddenly feel like I'm viewing life through a tunnel and my heart seems to slow down with each beat sounding louder than the previous one.

When he doesn't say anything else, I place it on the island next to my laptop and take a long sip of my ice water to calm myself down.

Tin finally looks over his shoulder at me before his eyes catch sight of where I placed the Property cut he gave me.

"Or are you thinking of heading out?" he asks, not for the first time, as his face suddenly turns as cold as ice.

"You have to ask me. Nicely." I specify what I need from him, keeping my eyes locked on him and praying he'll give me the words I long for. I know he's used to living life on his terms, but if he wants me by his side, he has to make room for me.

"Be my Ol' Lady, Paige?" Tin asks, starting to look a little pale under his tan skin. He manages to sound exasperated before he shoves the bag of apples into the corner of the counter and turns to fully face me, placing his hands flat on the island. "I never considered asking any other woman that. I'll be good to you, even if I am a cranky asshole. Sometimes. We both have things in our past that we're not proud of, but I know we can build a different future."

"Do you love me?" I ask, past the lump in my throat.

He sucks in his breath when I ask that question and closes his eyes briefly before stalking around the island to me.

Stopping just next to me, he lifts the cut up and looks me in the eyes.

"I love you, Paige Kyle," Tin says, holding the cut open so I can slide my right arm in if I choose to accept it.

Accept him.

Keeping the mask on my face, I slide my arm in and he helps me with the other side. Then I turn back to my laptop before asking, "What do you want for dinner?"

Next, I scream as he yanks me off the stool and hoists me over his shoulder, spanking me for good measure.

"Fucking witch. You've had me sick to my stomach all day," he grumbles as he walks to our bedroom, and I bite down on the knuckle of my thumb to keep from laughing. "Then she says, 'What do you want for dinner?'."

"I sicken you? And you think that means we'd be good together?" I sass back as I find myself being carefully laid on my back and pinned to the bed.

"No more running, Paige. We're together now,

you and me," Tin says with all seriousness, and I arch my neck up so I can kiss him.

"I'm going to want a baby or two," I say, giving him fair warning about my expectations, and he smiles at me like he knew I was going to say that.

"Fine. As long as there aren't any twins, I'm totally on board with that," he agrees, giving me a quick kiss and I gasp against his mouth.

"Why did you say that?" I squeal, trying to sit up, but can't with his hands still holding my wrists to the bed. "Don't you know what you've done?"

"Paige," he starts. "You know damn well I don't believe in any of that hocus pocus shit."

"No, now we're going to have like triplets or sextuplets, and it's all your fault!"

"Well, we're definitely going to have sex, but I'm fairly certain that me laying down the law is not how multiple births occur," he cleverly replies to my fear of sextuplets, laughing as he starts kissing my neck and I can't help but to shift and give him better access.

"That's what you think," I sigh in response, more interested in our foreplay than arguing over the fact that he basically just cursed us with a huge family.

When he leans back to take his clothes off, I slide out of my pajama bottoms and lift my T-shirt up. There's no way I'm ready to take my cut off.

TIN

"Tin." I think now's a good a time as any to broach the next topic.

"Yes, Ol' Lady," he responds, grinning wickedly at me, but I just roll my eyes and click my tongue at that.

"Will you tell me your name now?" I coyly ask, looking down at my nipples as I roll them between my fingers.

He once again covers me with his body and thoroughly kisses me. Just when I think he's going to ignore my question, his lips trace their way across my cheek and he whispers his first and last name into my ear.

My eyes shoot open and dart to meet his. Any thought that he was kidding flies out the window when I see his expression, so I nonchalantly just say, "Oh!" before he thrusts inside of me and that subject loses its importance, for now.

EPILOGUE

Tin

Closing her laptop and setting it aside, I smile at her where she sits across the room from me.

Holding up my arms, I silently invite her to join me now that I've finished reading her new release.

"Do you like it?" she asks, straddling me.

"I really fucking do," I tell her. "Some of that hasn't happened though."

"Well, it is fiction, babe."

"It doesn't have to be," I respond, my hands traveling from her thighs to her cup her tits. "Actually, I think we should try that one thing now."

"Which *thing*?" she asks, trying so hard to look innocent.

"Oh, you know which thing!"

I reach up and tear her shirt down the center; the smile she gives me perfectly conveys: Game On.

Paige

"They're perfect," I whisper to Piper as I stand over the basinet that easily holds both of her babies.

"Don't worry about waking them, once they fall asleep you could play the drums in here and they wouldn't stir," she tells me, smiling even as she shakes her head at them.

"Why don't you get some sleep and I'll watch them," I offer, not exactly sure about what I'm doing, but doubt taking care of them can be that hard.

"They'll be fine with the monitor, I just want to complete the finishing touches in their room," she says, turning to make sure the device is turned on. "Why don't you help me?"

Between the two of us, we hang and arrange the gifts she had received for the babies and holds the rocking chair as I balance on it to hang the mobile I made for my nephews. Piper's face lights up as the stones catch the sunlight and the walls around us dance with the light and rainbows that are cast through them.

"Thank you," she says, and her smile brightening up the room even more. "You can always have it back, when it's your turn."

"Whoa," I say, holding my hand up to ward off her thoughts. "We aren't there yet. Besides, Tin and I are going to spend the summer riding up to Alaska."

From the glint in her eyes, I can tell she's got a zinger coming but she swallows it when we hear the front door opening.

"Hey! We're back," Parker's voice bellows through the house to announce that he and Tin have arrived with dinner.

"I'm starving! Can you hit the light?" she asks, rushing toward the hallway.

I'd tease her about that, except she is providing sustenance for two tiny humans, so I let it pass. Before I turn off the light, I take another look at the mobile and grin at the centerpiece.

That damn broach finally came to good use.

THE END

THANK YOU

To Sapphire Knight, I appreciate that you didn't take a restraining order out against me when I constantly 'checked in' about getting into MMM19 and I'm so excited to be a part of this signing also. XO

To Scarlett Black, one of several friends I made at 2019's MMM signing. When I realized where my characters were going to be, I had to give a shout out to her Battle Born MC, Tank & Kat in particular. Check her out!

To Tina Workman, thank you for adopting me at my first MMM and making my world so much brighter.

To Adriano, sorry for all the nights I barely make it to bed. Thank you for always listening to me talk about 'people' who don't exist outside of my head or these pages and for being my biggest cheerleader. I love you, Goose.

To Brenda Keller, your covers are almost as beautiful as your smile! Thank you for all you do behind the scenes.

To Christopher, thanks for working with me for the perfect shot!

ADDITIONAL WORKS FROM M. MERIN

Northern Grizzlies MC Series:

Jasper (Book 1)

Flint (Book 2)

Gunner (Book 3)

Charlie (Book 4)

Michaels (Book 5)

Betsy (Book 6)

Shade (Book 7)

Chains: Northern Grizzlies MC Short I

Wrench: Northern Grizzlies MC Short II

Royal Bastards MC, Flagstaff Chapter:

Axel (Book 1)

Declan (Book 2)

Diesel (Book 3)

Snowed In, A Royal Bastard Surprise (Book 4)

Wolfman (Book 5)

Also Available:

Black Hills Shifters Books 2 & 4

His Touch

Ever After Series: Dark Ever After (Book 1)

& Julia's Journey (Book 2)

Molotov Brothers: The Reluctant King (Book 1)

Kal: A Rogue Enforcers Novella

The Weight of Blood (A Cuffed and Pinched Duet)

MMM Mayhem Makers Collaboration

Me'ansome: Grave Knights MC (Book 1)

Tin: Grave Knights MC (Book 2)

Made in the USA
Middletown, DE
30 May 2023